Catastrophe in the Kitchen

Purrfect Travel Companion

Book One

Rosie Pease

PAISLEY PRESS BOOKS
WEST WARWICK, RHODE ISLAND

To the many amazing travel cats and their people I've found across social media. Thank you for sharing your journeys.

CHAPTER ONE

I t had been two weeks since I adopted my cat, Trubbs, short for Trouble, from a cat café during an investigation into a man's death while I was on a bus trip.

It had been one week since I learned Trubbs could talk.

Yes, really talk. And only to me. Sometimes he'd meow or make some other noise while we chatted when others were around, but they could only hear that. Little more than a baby meow to them. But I heard everything else.

I haven't decided yet if it's all in my head. Both how he could talk and how I could hear him.

My parents, who I rented an apartment from in the basement of their house, said he was a quiet cat. Clearly, they weren't able to hear him. They must have had some good insulation soundproofing the main part of the house from the apartment below. Because beyond the talking, Trubbs didn't live quietly either. He lived up to his name and then some. My new exercise routine, not that I'd had one before, was cleaning up after my cat—righting things on the counter, picking things up from the floor that he'd knocked off shelves, tiptoeing around the occasional broken object on my way to the closet to grab the broom or vacuum.

And when he wasn't causing a mess in the house, he was off gallivanting in the neighborhood somewhere. Causing trouble, no doubt. I'd wanted him to be an inside cat. He'd refused. Considering he had figured out several ways to escape the apartment, one I was still trying to figure out, I didn't have much choice in the matter. Though that didn't keep me from trying to convince him otherwise.

"I'm perfectly capable of taking care of myself," he told me yet again as he hopped to my nightstand, knocking the book that had been there off. "I'll look both ways before crossing the street."

Looking at the book on the floor as I stood a few feet away at my dresser, I didn't feel super confident about his answer. Trubbs didn't even look to see where he was going before he jumped to wherever it was. He didn't need to know I doubted his abilities, though. "That takes care of cars, but what about coyotes?" They didn't roam in the main parts of town, but people closer to the forest north of us had reported sightings.

"Pretty sure they'll freak out and leave me alone once I yell at them."

After pulling out my shirt, I closed the drawer a little too hard in reaction to his statement. "You can talk to coyotes?"

"If I want to. Just like how I can talk to you."

"Why *can* you talk to me?" I pulled my plain teal T-shirt over my head. My boss didn't like us wearing graphic tees to work, even if our aprons would cover the entire design. "I'm not a witch, am I?"

He made a funny noise that I hadn't heard him make yet. I assumed it to be a laugh, but it came out as a half snort mixed with his squeak of a meow. "Goodness, no. At least not in the way you're thinking. Maybe one of your ancestors was."

I slid my arms into the sleeves one at a time. "Have you tried talking to my parents? They say you're quiet, and I know better."

"Completely unreceptive." He flicked his tail.

"So how can one of my ancestors be a witch if my parents can't talk to you?" I picked up the black pants I had already laid out on the bed. Covered in cat fur. This was my life now. I'd have to run the lint roller over them once they were on. My boss had warned me about excessive cat fur on my clothes. Repeatedly.

Trubbs licked a paw and brought it up over his ear. "Might be one of those recessive gene things."

I blinked at him a moment as I slipped on my pants. "How do you know about recessive genes?" Just what type of cat was he?

He paused in his cleaning, his tongue partially out. "We had a lot of students come into the catio to study. One, in particular, would read out loud. Picked it up from her."

In a situation where nothing made sense, this probably made the most sense.

I headed to my living room where I'd left my shoes, having kicked them off when I got home the afternoon before. Trubbs followed me, scampering up onto the recliner.

"So do all the cats at the cat café know about recessive genes and whatever else people may have talked about while they sat there and studied?" I stuffed my foot into one of my shoes.

"Well, sure, some do. Not all of them are regular cats." He circled the seat cushion three times before sitting down.

The next shoe needed to be tied again, and I stooped to take care of it. "Regular cats?"

"Yeah, cats like me aren't normal cats. Didn't you notice the name of the cat café?"

I thought back to my bus trip that resulted in Trubbs coming into my life. "Yeah, Feline Familiar, wasn't it?"

"That's it. *Familiar*. As in witch's familiar."

"But we agreed I'm not a witch."

"You aren't. But plenty of others who come in are."

"So why me?" It was not the first time I'd asked the question.

"I was so ready to get out of there." It was not the first time he'd used that as an answer either.

"That has nothing to do with me, though."

He flicked his tail again. I'd come to interpret it as his version of a shrug. "You had a good way about you from the moment you walked into the café. Thought you'd be going places. Wasn't exactly wrong about that."

"Well, the only place I'm going now is to work." I glanced at the clock on the stove. "Oh, sugar. I gotta go. Stay out of trouble today!"

I should have listened to my own advice.

Chapter Two

I hurried to my apartment door, then grabbed my bag off the side table next to the entry and left, pulling the door closed behind me. Had this been how Trubbs was escaping? In addition to being a talking cat, could he also use a regular doorknob? It wasn't like he had to use a key. No one bothered to lock up in Wisteria Falls. It was a safe, small town. Everyone knew everyone here.

I made it to work with no time to spare. Unfortunately, in my boss's eyes, that practically made me late.

"Look what the cat dragged in," he commented as I scooted across the kitchen to stow my bag in my cubby and grab an apron for the day. Purple. Like the tile floors in the bakeshop. The place had been renovated in the early 2000s, and the tile had played up the fun designs and bright colors of Flour Power bakery. Now, the floors, like the rest of the shop, had seen better days. I remembered coming into the bakery as a kid, back before my boss owned it, and had loved the sixties tie-dye vibe. I'd been so excited about getting a job here after culinary school because I'd had such fond memories of this place. All my birthday cakes had been from here growing up. This was the place to go. Not any longer. Although we still did okay, every day it seemed like fewer people were coming in, and Gio's attitude was taking a hit.

We'd all felt the brunt of it.

Although my parents had a cat, my not living with them directly meant the few hairs I picked up during family dinners twice a week were easily taken care of in the wash. The moment Gio noticed I had cat fur on my required black pants my first day back at work after getting Trubbs, he'd lost it.

"You cannot come into work looking like that," he'd said at the time.

I remembered looking down and seeing cat fur, but not an overwhelming amount of it. I'd seen more on Roni, whose jacket in the winter was covered with long tufts of fur from her dog. Somehow that wasn't a problem.

"Sorry. I forgot what having a cat was like," I'd told him. "You must know how attracted they are to solid-color clothes, especially black ones." I swore he'd told me he had a cat once, but that was years ago.

"You forgot? That's no excuse. Maybe next week I'll forget to pay you."

That was when I started using the lint roller before work. Something I was now kicking myself for forgetting to do, even after I told Trubbs I needed to. Hopefully Gio wouldn't notice.

I smiled at Stacey and Roni, the other two bakers in the kitchen, as I passed them. There had been one more, Adam, but he'd been let go the week prior. Stacey rolled her eyes at Gio's statement to me. She'd been the one to suggest the lint roller. It worked for her.

With as much forced cheer as I could muster, I greeted

my boss, ignoring his comment completely. "Morning, Gio. How are you today?" I wouldn't let him get to me.

Once upon a time, he wasn't like this. Gio had been excited I was double majoring in culinary arts, with a concentration on baking and pastry, and travel and tourism. He'd practically offered me a job to work in the kitchen when I got my acceptance letter. I'd already been working in the shop on weekends and during school breaks.

He wasn't like this when I first graduated either. My first year had been great. Then, during a week when I was away for a beach vacation, he'd been surprised with a divorce. I doubted he had smiled since. I tried to cut him some slack, but that was three years ago now, and his demeanor hadn't improved. If anything, it had gotten worse.

"Same old. Same old." Gio punched down some bread dough that had likely been rising overnight.

I hopped onto my workstation next to the stove, happy to mix up some new lemon curd for the lemon square bars. "How about we throw some blueberries into this today? You know how well lemon and blueberry go together."

"No blueberries."

"But it's the height of the season. They're fresh and local and cheap." I hoped highlighting the cost would spark some interest in him, although he never wanted to try anything new.

"And that means everyone will be doing something with blueberries. No," he grumbled. "Let's stick to what we know."

I filled the double boiler with water and then placed it on the stove. "Are you saying we don't know blueberries?" Which was impossible because we made fabulous blueberry muffins and pies.

He let out a rumbly sigh. "I'm saying that we don't need to reinvent anything."

"But we won't be reinventing anything," I said as I clicked the burner on and then cracked three eggs to get the three yolks and one egg white the recipe required. "Blueberries and lemons have been paired together for ages. Why don't you try anything new anymore?"

He used to once. Back before his mood turned sourer than the lemons I was about to turn into the most amazing curd. I should have just added the blueberries myself without asking. He still hadn't picked up on my improvements to the curd over a year ago. I doubted he'd had any of the sweets we baked in years. No one could be so unhappy with cookies in their diet. A good friend once told me that cookies made everything better, and I agreed.

"Because I like things the way they are." Unfortunately, things *the way they are* were not good. Without innovation in our menu, the bakery had become stale. People wanted stuffed cupcakes with innovative decorations or cookies the size of their hand or a wider bread variety. Gio wanted none of it.

By the time I'd cut and cubed the six tablespoons of butter required for the curd, the water had started to boil. I reduced the heat, then added my dry ingredients, lemon juice, and eggs to the top layer of the double boiler. "But what if it could be better?"

Behind me, Gio's dough hit his workstation hard. "Why do you want to change things?" he asked from much closer than his station.

Not looking at him because I had to whisk the curd continuously so the egg wouldn't curdle as it heated—no one would want lemony scrambled eggs on a shortbread crust—I replied, "Because I remember how great this place used to be."

"Oh, you mean when I didn't own it, right?"

"You know that's not what I meant. I've been here a long time, Gio. Been coming here since I was a kid. Yes, some of that was before you took over from Max, but you're the one who motivated me all through school and gave me my first experience working in a bakery. This place, you, and everyone here mean a lot to me. Why wouldn't I want to do my part to help it succeed?"

"Flour Power doesn't need your help." He was even closer now.

"What are you saying?" The curd had thickened, so I pulled the double boiler off the burner, turned that off, and then set the pots on a trivet at my workstation. It was the first time I'd looked at Gio since getting here this morning. Behind him, Stacey stood with a blue piping bag in hand, eyes wide, frozen instead of frosting the cupcakes in front of her.

"You can pick up your last check on Friday."

"That's it?" I dropped the butter chunks into the curd to melt before finally turning toward Gio. "You're just going to fire me for trying to bring some life back into this place?"

He stood scowling at me with his arms crossed. "I'm firing you for changing recipes without my okay. Don't think I haven't noticed you using a whole egg instead of two more egg yolks in the curd."

"It makes the curd thicker and helps it stay better once you cut the lemon squares. I've been doing it for months, and no one has complained."

"And now you won't be doing it any longer. You can put your apron in the bin."

"The butter still needs to be whisked in," I told Stacey calmly. Then I yanked off my apron as I stormed past Gio on my way out of the kitchen. I slammed both it and the bakery key onto the shop counter. "You're going to regret doing this," I called out to him before leaving out the front door.

In hindsight, I probably shouldn't have said that.

Chapter Three

Furious over my firing, I drove to the next town over and stopped at the bakery there for a stuffed cupcake and a delicious latte. Although I'd been hearing great things about it, I hadn't gone out of loyalty to Gio. That, and it would have frustrated me even more to see how much more Flour Power could be if Gio would only allow it.

Instead of allowing it, Gio stifled it, and I'd become the second person he'd fired in less than a few weeks.

Once the caffeine and sugar hit my system, I felt better and then slowly made my drive back to Wisteria Falls. I wasn't ready to go home, though. It was still too early, and I wasn't ready for Mom's questions about why I was home when I was supposed to be working. She knew Gio kept turning down my ideas and that his attitude had soured over the years, but I had to come up with a plan first. Update my resume. Figure out where I could apply for jobs. Then I'd be able to answer her questions and those my father would no doubt have for me too.

As I crossed the town line, I turned north onto Greenhouse Road toward our botanical park. Aptly named Wisteria Falls, the park's main attraction was beautiful vining purple flowers that cascaded from the top of cliffs down into a small lake. Although the height of their season had been a couple months ago, the botanical gardens boasted some later-blooming varieties that were still flowering amid the greenery of the earlier kinds. That was on top of all the other flowers they had along multiple walking trails, and now, in midsummer, those were in abundance.

I chose the hike. For the mostly paved paths I'd be taking, my bakery shoes were more than sufficient. They had to be with as much time I spent on my feet as I did. Did. Huh. I wondered if I'd end up at some desk job somewhere. I'd have to get an entirely new wardrobe if that happened. Doubted too many offices in town wanted t-shirts, black jeans, and sneakers to be worn in the office.

One thing at a time, I told myself as I got out of the car and started my trek, my phone at the ready so I could take photos. Might as well turn this into a blog post to say I did something productive with my unexpected time off.

"Morning, Meredith! How are you and that cat of yours?" Robin Clark asked me, a pair of binoculars around her neck. "I think I saw him palling around with one of my ferals."

"He refuses to be an indoor cat. Escapes no matter what I try to do." I chuckled. "At least he's making friends."

She smiled at me, then waved over my shoulder at someone else. "Living up to his name, then."

"You bet." Robin knew all about Trubbs's antics. She'd been on the bus trip with me when I ended up getting Trubbs. She and her husband had helped me bring him home from the cat café. "What are you doing here today?"

"Local bird watching meetup. I may be a crazy cat lady,

but I've always loved birds. I come here since I can't put feeders out at my house. That wouldn't be fair to them."

At that moment, the people Robin had waved to joined us, binoculars in their hands. I did a double take, and the older sisters giggled.

"Aunt Bertha, Aunt Betty. Sorry, I'm not used to seeing you two so . . ."

"Athletic?" Aunt Bertha provided.

I nodded. We could go with that. I was more used to seeing the Aunts of Wisteria Falls (whose aunts they actually were, I wasn't sure anyone knew) in flowing all-black or jewel-toned clothes with lots of beads and bangles. They put on an amazing Halloween party and a full yard and house display during the season, but they themselves seemed to live as if it were that time of year all the time, minus the decorations.

"I didn't even recognize you," I confessed, studying the two.

"It gets dreadfully hot after too long of a walk in our usual attire, especially in the heat like this," Aunt Betty said.

Aunt Bertha stuck out her leg and made a show of her purple leggings. "I admit these are rather comfortable. I can see why you young people like to wear them for more than yoga."

I chuckled. "They're also good for sleeping in."

The sisters looked appalled, Aunt Bertha bringing her hand to her chest. "Oh Goddess, no. I can't imagine that would be comfortable."

"Too restricting," her sister agreed. "But perhaps when we go gather materials to make our brooms . . ."

Robin waved behind me again. "Looks like the rest of the group is here." She turned toward me. "You have a lovely walk, Meredith. Maybe next time you could come birding with us if you bring some binoculars with you."

"Oh, I don't have any."

"Well, we have extra pairs somewhere in the house," Aunt Betty replied. "We'll start keeping a set in the car should you ever wish to join us."

I nodded politely but made no promises. It did sound somewhat interesting, however. "And you all have a lovely time bird watching. Hoping to see anything in particular?"

"Oh, I'd love to see the ravens again. Such marvelous birds," Aunt Bertha gushed.

It wasn't the answer I'd been expecting, but it fit the sisters perfectly. Goddess? Brooms? Ravens? Just who were those aunts?

"Well, I hope you find them again."

The three walked away, tittering like birds themselves. I smiled at the trio and the group beyond them waiting for them to join, then waved one final time at them all before turning in the opposite direction. The three women had unknowingly helped me out in a big way, banishing the last of my anger over being fired and clearing my head to allow me to think about my next steps.

The first of which was taking pictures of flowers and landscapes.

Chapter Four

The reality of being unemployed hit me two days later when I realized I'd be picking up my last check the next morning. I'd land a job eventually, but what if the places where I'd already applied took a while to get back to me about interviews and even longer to decide who to hire?

Guess I'd have to dip into my travel fund if things got too tight.

"You should work on your blog," Trubbs suggested after I'd finished yet another chick flick.

"I finished all my posts for the next month." I posted two a week. Sadly, I didn't travel enough yet to justify more.

Trubbs nudged my side in the direction of my laptop. "Have you talked about the cat café yet? I know you wanted to."

I grabbed the remote and clicked the button to shut off the TV. "Only in passing about it being where I got you."

He crawled up behind my shoulders to sit between them and the chair. "But you have more material for it. You took photos of that chocolate mouse."

The mousse mouse. It was delicious. "Right. I'm sure I could work it in."

Trubbs rolled to his back, giving his paws access to my ponytail. "You had a whole plan for once you introduced me, remember? The Purrfect Travel Companion? Why don't you take the time to rebrand? Take me back to that park you went to with the birds or something. It would be fun."

"You don't want to take yourself? I hear you've been getting around. Robin's seen you at her house, and she doesn't exactly live close." I pulled my lap desk over toward me, then opened my computer.

The movement caused Trubbs to shift slightly. He swatted my ponytail. "I like traveling as much as you do. Come on . . . You know I did great in the car."

"Will you wear a harness and a leash? A collar too? I know you've rejected the collar idea when you go outside alone." Much to my chagrin. I'd asked him to wear one when I realized there was no way for me to stop him from going outside on his own. At least he was microchipped just in case.

"You know I'd just lose it after a day or two, and you'd have to buy me another one. I may be able to talk, but I'm still a cat after all."

"That didn't answer my question." There was a knock at the door, and after moving my laptop, I went to answer it. Trubbs unceremoniously flopped to the cushion I'd vacated.

"Fine, fine. I'll wear your human contraptions if it means I get to see the sites," he called after me as I pulled the door open to reveal my mom holding a box.

Usually happy to give me my privacy unless invited inside, she peeked around me. "Is Trubbs okay? He seems a bit put out." I had no idea what she had heard instead of him talking to me.

"He's unhappy I moved from the chair. What's up?"

She held out the box. "This came for you. It was missing the apartment number so ended up on our doorstep. Should have gone through the mail."

My dad, being our mail carrier, would have brought it to the right door. I glanced at the sender's address as Mom placed the box in my hands. "Oh, good. My candy."

"More specialty candy for you to review? I'm only going to say it once, but you need to watch your spending." I knew she was only looking out for me, but I was well aware of my financial situation. Always had been, even before getting fired.

"Mom," I started, exaggerating the *ah* sound. "This is the candy the cops from Snowhaven had to replace when I was on that bus trip. It's not new."

"Oh, well, that was nice of them."

"They kinda had to." I walked over to the counter in my tiny kitchen a few feet away and then set the box on top of it. Turning back to my mom, I asked, "You want to come in?"

She shook her head. "No, I'll leave you to whatever you were doing. Just wanted to give you the box. Any job leads today?"

"No luck so far, but I'm going to rebrand my blog. New name, new theme, all that stuff. Trubbs did so well in the car ride home that I want to try taking him to a couple places. See how that goes. I think people will love it. I follow a lot of doggie travelers, but fewer people take cats places."

Mom brightened. "Did you see that article about the kitty mountain climber?" She was always finding cute things on the internet. If I wasn't her daughter, she'd no doubt end up following me on my blog if I had a cat on it.

"I have. I should go back and read it again. Maybe do some research and find out what sort of gear his owner takes with them when they go out."

"I'm sure I have it bookmarked." She spun on her heels,

then took a few steps toward the front of the house. "I'll send it to you when I find it."

Chapter Five

I spent the rest of the evening fixing my old travel blog and turning it into The Purrfect Travel Companion. Trubbs granted me the permission of having a mini photoshoot with him so that I could introduce him *propurrly* and create a new logo. As much as he refused to wear a collar on his own, it turned out he didn't mind bandanas or sunglasses. Mine made him look goofy, but I'd have to get my hand on some toddler ones. Those would fit better.

By the following morning, my redesign was complete with a new domain name in place, and I was feeling pretty proud of myself.

The only thing dampening my mood was having to go pick up my last paycheck.

Fortunately, I was still used to the early hours. I wanted to get this over with as quickly as possible. Then I could come back and launch the new site. I'd taken it down so no one would see it while it was still a work in progress.

I glanced at Trubbs on the bed as I got dressed. "You don't have to come with me, you know."

"Sure I do. Think of me as moral support." He licked his paw and started rubbing it along his face.

I eyed the silver-white tabby. "Moral support?"

"Okay, not really. I know you're more than capable of handling things on your own. It can't get much worse than it already is. You've already been fired after all. But you're going to have to get used to me traveling with you and walking around with you, so why not get started now? Think of it as a way to drum up interest in your new blog."

"You're really smart, you know that?"

He froze midlick, paw raised. "I thought we figured that out already."

I chuckled. "Just what else did you learn at that café while people read out loud?"

He squinted slowly at me. "I was plenty smart before the café, thank you very much."

"Sorry, didn't mean to offend you."

"It's all right. I'll let it go this time." He walked up to me and then bumped his head against my hip, leaving a patch of cat fur on my black pants as he moved to sit back down.

I wasn't touching the cat fur. No doubt Gio would see it when I showed up, and that wasn't my problem anymore. He couldn't do a thing about it. That satisfied me in some small way. We'd been on good terms, him and I, until after I got home from my last trip. Who knew the invisible line I'd unknowingly crossed in our working relationship was cat fur?

"Guess we should get going," I said, heading to the door. "I don't have a harness or leash yet for you, so—"

"I'll stay close." Trubbs hopped off the bed with a loud thump, followed by a whoomp. I turned back to see my top blanket half behind him and half on top of him. He scrambled out from under it, then easily caught up to me.

As we reached the door to my apartment, I slid my feet

into my sneakers, then grabbed my bag. "And try not to cause any trouble on the way."

I opened the door, and Trubbs stepped outside. "I make no promises."

He led the way to my car and hopped in after me once I sat down. Then he tried to shimmy between me and the seat as if it was my recliner.

"Oh, no, not in the car. If anything ever happened, you'd be squished."

"Fine." He balanced on my shoulder for a moment before jumping to the passenger seat, then propped himself up to look out the window, which started to open. Trubbs jumped back and turned to look at me, his tail's circumference more than doubling. "What is that magic?"

Stifling a giggle at how poofy his tail had gotten, I replied, "Automatic windows. You pressed the button." I'd have to remember to lock them whenever he was in the car.

"Maybe you *are* a witch."

"Nope, they come standard in cars now." Though he probably hadn't been in many cars to know that. When we'd come home from Snowhaven, the air conditioner had been on. The windows never went down for him to see how they worked.

He approached the slightly open window, nose twitching and tail slightly less poofy. "I might like this. Lots of smells this way."

I started the car, then put it into reverse, and we slowly backed out of the driveway and into the road. "I won't open it more than that with you free roaming in the car like you are."

He said nothing as he continued to sniff out the window.

"So where were you before you ended up at the cat café? You weren't there super long, and according to the paperwork I was given, they estimated you were about three years old."

"I'd rather not talk about it, but I'm two and a half."

I thought about pressing him on the issue but decided against it. We were already pulling up to the bakery. On good days, it was close enough to walk to. We could have today since it was nice out, but as I was just running in, I figured I could take Trubbs to the pet store with me to get a harness after this and then somewhere fun. Maybe the botanical park like he'd suggested.

After throwing the car into park, I cut the engine, then got out.

Trubbs followed me once again.

"You can't come in with me," I told him as we approached the door to Flour Power. "I may have gotten fired, but I don't want them to get closed down for a health violation because you've been in there."

"Got it. I'll wait outside." The large plate-glass windows would give him ample ability to see inside the shop.

He stood with his front paws against the glass. I momentarily thought about telling him to get down, but Gio could handle cleaning up the tiny smudge prints if he wanted to. I tried the door, expecting it to already be unlocked as Gio waited for the others to get here, but it wasn't.

"Huh."

Trubbs glanced at me. "What?"

"It's locked." I rang the doorbell. Maybe he'd come in from the back, not that he ever had before. Nothing. I rang it again in case he'd stepped into the bathroom or was in the cooler. Again nothing.

"Stay here." I went around to the side of the building to peer inside one of the back windows, then quickly returned to get Trubbs. "I need your help." I was too short to see in the window by myself, but if Trubbs could climb up onto the ledge, he'd have no problem.

"Aren't you glad I came along?"

"Yes," I said, waving him around the corner.

He trotted toward me, and I explained to him what I wanted. Then I picked him up, and with the agility expected of a cat, he leapt from my shoulder to the windowsill.

"I see him," Trubbs said. "He's sitting down."

"Sitting down? Where?" That wasn't like Gio. That man never sat. Too much energy—most of it angry.

"On the floor by a big silver door."

What a weird spot. "That's the walk-in refrigerator."

"He must have spilled something."

"Why do you say that?" Thinking better of it, I didn't stay to hear the answer. I rushed back to the front of the building, dread blooming in my stomach. Before reaching the door, I was already digging through my bag for something that could pick the lock. This bag had everything. Eventually, I slid an expired credit card from my wallet, then used the entire wallet to tap the credit card between the lock and the plate. Gio had talked about replacing the old lock at some point, but in a town where no one bothered to lock their houses, it hadn't been a priority for him.

Finally the lock gave out, and I pushed my way inside the bakery and bolted into the kitchen.

The light was on, the ovens heated and ready for the day, dough proofing at one of the stations.

And Gio on the floor.

Dead.

CHAPTER SIX

I raced to Gio's side. If he was alive and unconscious, he needed help fast.

Unfortunately, there were no signs of life. I bit back a cry as I pulled my hands away from his neck, having found no pulse. Sure, our last encounter with one another hadn't been the greatest, but I never would have wished the man dead.

I grabbed my phone from my pocket, then quickly dialed 911. The dispatcher informed me that officers were already on their way.

"Already on their way?" I mumbled as I hung up. How was that possible? It didn't sit right with me.

"Are you okay? I heard you cry out," Trubbs shouted through the kitchen door. I was both touched and unsurprised that he'd run inside for me.

"Trubbs, get back outside. We can't have you contaminating the scene any more than it already is."

"Scene?"

"Yeah, crime scene." I stood back up and pressed the

camera app on my phone. "Gio's dead, and I don't think this was an accident."

"But I want to help." Trubbs let out a long whining meow.

"Your best help will be to wait outside for me. I'll be there as soon as I can."

"Okay," he said, his tone completely changed from moments before. "Cops will be here soon."

As if on cue, the sound of fast-approaching sirens cut through the silence of the morning. Knowing I didn't have long, I snapped as many pictures of the kitchen as I could from where I was standing. It would have to do.

The sirens went silent, and within moments, the door to the kitchen slammed open. I jumped, nearly dropping my phone.

"Step back from the body," an officer bellowed, his gun drawn.

I thrust my hands into the air, keeping hold of my phone. "I found him like this," I cried. My gaze darted to the phone in my hand. "I just called for an ambulance and was told that you were already on your way."

"Take a step back, miss," the officer ordered, his gun still drawn but his voice calmer.

Doing as he requested, my voice shook as I said, "I had to see if he was okay. I haven't touched anything other than Gio's neck to check for a pulse. There isn't one."

I squinted, trying to figure out if I knew the officer. I knew everyone in town. Or thought I did. This face was new to me.

"What's your name?" the officer asked.

"Meredith Duffy."

"Mer?" This voice sounded cautious, but it was one I knew, and my shoulders sagged in relief.

"Jay? You get a new partner?"

The officer who'd had his gun drawn on me lowered his weapon only slightly. He kept his gaze trained on me as the door to the kitchen opened once more to reveal my best friend's older brother.

"New last week," Jay answered with an unsure smile on his handsome face. I'd had such a crush on him as a kid. "Patrick, this is my sister's best friend. You can put your gun away. She works here. Mer, what happened?" His smile fell as he took in the scene.

Jay's partner holstered his weapon. Now that a gun wasn't pointed at me, I lowered my hands and then slipped my phone into my pocket, exiting out of the camera app in the process. They didn't need to know I'd taken photos.

"He was like this when I got here. The door was locked, so I picked it and let myself in."

"Why didn't you use your key?"

"I don't have one." I could barely look him in the eye as I added, "Had to turn it in when I got fired on Monday."

Jay's eyes widened. "You got fired? How? Your baked goods are wicked good."

"Insubordination. But I was only trying to make things better." I drew my lips to the side as I gently shrugged.

"And you couldn't just knock?" Patrick—no clue if that was his first or last name—asked. "Maybe ring a bell?"

I shook my head. "Tried. Multiple times. But I saw the light on and knew he had to be inside because it's close to opening. Something felt wrong to me. Obviously for good reason."

"You didn't think to call when you were trying to get inside?"

"I called once I got in here. You can check with Nancy at dispatch. She said you were already on your way. Why were you on your way?"

Jay eyed me as if I should have known the answer, and his lips curled into a slight grin. "For someone trying to break in."

A light went off in my head. "Ooh . . . Whoops." I chided myself for not calling the cops as I tried to get inside the bakery.

"So if you were fired," Patrick started, "why were you here?"

"Officer . . ."

"Owens."

"Officer Owens, I was here to pick up my last check. Wanted to get it out of the way early to avoid the others. Oh my goodness, where are Stacey and Roni? They should be here by now."

"Officers have them outside," Jay assured me. "Stopped them from coming in the back."

"Good. That's good. I'm glad they're okay," I said, exhaling hard. Losing Gio was bad enough. What if they had been in here? Would they be dead now too, or would that have saved Gio? "Am I in trouble?"

Jay shook his head. "You were trying to help someone you thought needed it."

Officer Owens shot him a look. "We'll figure that out later. For now, stay where you are. We don't need you disturbing the scene any more than you already have."

For the next several minutes, I stood still as Jay and his partner took photos. They were soon joined by two more officers, some CSI techs, and medics. The scene reminded me of the bus trip I'd been on a few short weeks ago, only this time, I was right in the middle of things from the start.

CHAPTER SEVEN

Finally I was given the all clear to step away from Gio's body so the investigative team could continue their work without me present.

Jay and his partner followed me into the shop portion of the bakery.

"We're going to need you to come to the station to answer a few questions," Jay said.

"I was going to take my cat to the botanical park, but I can take him home and swing by the station."

"Your cat?" Disbelief laced Officer Owens's voice.

I looked at Jay. "I rebranded my travel blog. Thought spicing it up with my new cat would be fun."

"Rita said you got a cat."

"Yeah," I said with a chuckle. "His name is Trouble."

"He wouldn't happen to be a silvery cat with black tabby stripes, would he?"

"You mean the one with his paws against the window right now?" I asked, pointing toward him. "That's him."

Jay's lips took on the slightest hint of a smile. "He must

really like you. He was meowing nonstop at the door when we got here. Had to do quite a bit of maneuvering to keep him outside."

"That would be Trubbs." He must have slipped inside without me noticing, but how had he gotten back out in time? That cat really could escape from anywhere. "He came in the car with me since I was planning on this being a quick stop."

"Too bad we can't interview cats," Officer Owens said under his breath.

"Wouldn't that be something?" I said, thinking that he'd be able to back me up if they could. It wasn't like the police would believe me if I tried to act as an interpreter right now.

I said goodbye to the officers, promising I would head to the station shortly, then headed outside.

Trubbs let his paws slide down the window before turning toward my car. I opened the passenger door for him, and he hopped in without a word.

Once I got in and started the car, I pulled out onto Main Street. "Sorry, Trubbs. Gotta put our plans on hold for a bit."

"What happened?" Although the window was open, all his focus was on me.

"Someone killed Gio. Now I have to go answer some questions at the station."

"What sort of questions?"

"Not the sort you want to be asked, that's for sure." We pulled up to the one stoplight in the heart of town. Solid red. Given the early morning hour, it had switched from being an overnight blinking light to a regular traffic light within the last few minutes. It was one of the first signs the town was waking up each day.

The time spent waiting at the light was just enough for me to start processing what had happened in the bakery kitchen.

"They found me with the body, Trubbs. I can't imagine that looks good for me."

"But you were only there to pick up your check."

The light turned green, and I made a left to head back toward home. "Yeah. My *last* paycheck. That could be seen as a motive." At his questioning glance, I explained to him what *motive* meant.

"So that means we have to find out who else could have a motive before the police think it's you. You can't go to jail. Who's going to make me those tuna treats?"

"I'll make a new batch when I get back from the station. That should last you a little while. Mom can't make them, but she can at least give them to you." My parents weren't culinarily inclined. They were a big reason why I'd started cooking in the first place. Although what my parents could cook had since turned into comfort food for me, as a kid, I got tired of eating the same pasta or hotdogs every night. I started making easy dinners for us all at seven. Nowadays, our twice-weekly family dinners were just as much for them as it was for me.

Trubbs flicked his tail. "Okay, I know I started it, but stop talking like you're going to get locked up. We're not going to let that happen. And to celebrate our success in keeping you out of jail, I can eat all those tuna treats in celebration. You can try some new candy or something. You don't need any more ice cream."

I'd gone through a pint a night after my firing. More sounded good right now. I hadn't had breakfast.

"You're going to take it easy on those treats, but yes, we can splurge a bit if I don't go to jail."

We pulled into the driveway, and Trubbs and I walked to the apartment. Not knowing how long I'd be at the station, I figured I should eat something.

I'd just grabbed an egg to fry out of the refrigerator when the door burst open. Once again, I jumped, but unlike earlier, I calmed quickly when I saw it was my mom . . . and my dad.

The fridge door closed hard as Mom pushed it in her rush to get to me. She threw her arms around me. "Oh, thank goodness you're safe. You weren't picking up your phone, and we started to think the worst."

"What's going on?" I pulled out of her grasp enough to set the egg on the counter.

She held me out at arm's length, refusing to let go. "Dolores called and woke us up this morning. She has a police scanner, you know, and she heard someone was trying to break into the bakery, and then while we were talking, there was all this chatter about there being a dead body. And well, she called because she didn't know you'd been fired, but we were so worried because we knew you'd gone to pick up your check."

Now Dad was looking me over.

"I'm fine. I promise," I told them, but it didn't ease their worried looks.

Mom finally stepped aside so Dad could get his hug. It was short and sweet, really the extent of his physical expression of concern. But the weight of his feelings was evident in his eyes as he asked, "What happened?"

As I worked around them to cook my egg, I recounted pulling up to the bakery to find it locked, then breaking in to discover Gio's body in the kitchen. I couldn't really tell them the part where Trubbs looked in through the kitchen window, prompting me to break in. Had that not happened, maybe I would have come back later, leaving Stacey or Roni to find Gio instead. It seemed Trouble was living up to his name and leading me right into the middle of it . . . though I had put him up to it.

"Are you in trouble for breaking into the bakery?"

I shrugged, then popped an English muffin into the toaster. "They didn't say. But now I'm having some breakfast because Jay asked me to go to the station to answer some questions for them."

Mom sighed with relief. "Oh, Jason, good." A smile played at her lips as she turned to my father to place a hand on his arm. "Everything will be fine."

Dad's grin matched hers as he nodded.

"What?" Why were my parents smiling? This was a horrible situation.

"He's always liked you," Mom said. "He's going to make sure you don't go to prison."

"Jay? Like me?" I blew a raspberry in disbelief. "I'm his sister's best friend."

"Giving you two a lot of history. Even his mom said so when you were kids."

The toaster popped. "Yeah, keyword being *kids*. We're far from that now." I pulled the muffin halves from the slots.

"Doesn't mean the feelings aren't still there. We see it at our summer barbeques. He's what, thirty and still single? A good-looking man like him?"

"There could be plenty of reasons why, Mom, and very few of them involve me." I slid the egg onto half the English muffin, closed it, then took a bite. With my mouth still full, I added, "If any."

"Now, now. Don't talk with your mouth full. You could choke."

I shooed my parents out of my kitchen. My breakfast needed cheese, and they'd been blocking the refrigerator. Jay? Like me? That was just silly. "Was there anything else?" I asked once I'd reassembled my sandwich.

Mom glanced at Dad. "No, but please put your ringer on. I tried calling you several times."

"I will after I leave the station. And I wouldn't have been able to pick up for you anyway given the situation."

"Jason would have let you." The smile was back on her face.

"Okay . . . you both can go now." I inclined my head toward the door and took another bite of breakfast.

Dad did as requested, but Mom came up to give me another hug. "Call me when you're done with questioning. I have money for bail."

My mouth dropped open, and I nearly lost the bit of muffin inside it. "Mom! I didn't do anything."

"No, no. I know you didn't kill Gio—oh, the poor man, even if he was a grouch—but you did break into the bakery. You admitted to that. Like I said, I'm sure Jason will have it taken care of, but just in case." She gave me one last squeeze. "I love you."

"Love you too, Mom."

Once she'd closed the door, I leaned back against the counter. There was no sense in getting comfortable when I had to head right back out. Trubbs jumped onto the counter next to me and bumped my side with his head.

"She might have bail money, but I'll just break you out if it comes to that."

I laughed. "You need your treats, I know."

"And they clearly need you," he replied, glancing at the door. "It's good to have people like that."

Popping the last bite of my sandwich into my mouth, I picked up my tabby cat and placed him over my shoulder. "Aww, I need you too, Trubbs."

"Hey . . . I didn't say . . ." I started scratching the side of his neck. "Okay, that is nice. He flopped his head against mine."

I turned, then kissed his head behind his ear. "Gotta put you down now."

"But I'm not done," he complained as I set him on the counter.

"Later." I chuckled. "Stay out of trouble."

"I think you could be in enough of it for the both of us. I'm staying put for once."

Chapter Eight

I pulled into the lot at the station. Unsure how long I'd be here for, I wasn't chancing parking in a timed spot out front. Last thing I needed today was a ticket for being in the station longer than the sign said I could be parked for.

Officer Tony Evans greeted me at the desk. I'd gone to school with him since preschool, our paths diverging only after high school graduation when I went to culinary school and he went to the police academy.

He gave me a sympathetic smile. No doubt he already knew.

"Please, don't look at me like that." I didn't need pity, but at least it told me no one suspected me of murder anymore.

"Sorry." His smile brightened. "It's good to see you, circumstances aside. Jay told me to be on the lookout for you. I'll let him know you're here."

"Thanks."

Pressing a button on the phone, he picked up the receiver. After a quick, "Mer's here," he set it down again.

"He'll be here in a minute."

I nodded.

He leaned forward. "How are you, really."

"It's not the first dead body I've seen, not even recently."

"Yeah, Rita mentioned something about that." Tony was married to my best friend, Jay's sister. I'd been in their wedding last year. "What a crazy trip that must have been."

"The last part sure was." But that fateful bus trip had led to me getting Trubbs, so death investigation aside, it had been more than worth it.

At that moment, Jay came walking down the hall. He slapped his hand down on the desk. "Thanks for keeping an eye on this one." He tried to give me a serious look as if I was in trouble—was I?—before splitting into a wide grin. He never could keep a straight face, not with me, and I relaxed at the sight, even if only slightly.

"She's all yours," Tony said, and the smile slipped from Jay's face. Tony gave him a look, but before I could call either of them on it, the phone rang. As Tony picked it up, he waved at me, and I turned to follow Jay back down the hall he'd come from.

The gravity of the situation weighed on me. I hadn't been past the front desk at the station since a field trip during elementary school and reminded Jay of that fact. I couldn't walk in silence. Not with Jay. It felt weird. We'd always been able to talk. I wasn't going to let Gio's death or Mom's claims about Jay liking me change that.

Speaking of moms . . . "How's your mom?" I asked. Jay, like me, lived in an apartment connected to his parents' house.

His smile returned, albeit a smaller one. "She's doing good. Shop's going well. Can only imagine she's going to get slammed with orders after what happened."

"Yeah, I imagine as the one florist in town, death is good for business."

"Glad to know your humor is intact." He opened a door to our left and held it for me so I could go in first.

"How chivalrous of you," I commented as I stepped through the doorway.

I'd hoped to get him to crack a grin once more, but his whole demeanor had shifted. "Policy."

I turned to give him a look, but someone else cleared their throat. I looked ahead of me and saw Patrick Owens. That explained it.

Officer Owens stood and motioned to the chair across the table from him. "Miss Duffy, thanks for coming in. Have a seat."

Jay followed me inside, then took the empty chair next to his partner. Owens pulled out a recorder, then set it on the table between the three of us. After pressing *record* and making an intro with the date and case file name and number, he had me state my full name. Then he dove right into questions.

I swallowed a lump in my throat. The recorder made this all seem that much more real, and I wished Trubbs was here behind me. It was true what they said about cats and lowering one's blood pressure, and mine was absolutely rising.

"Describe your relationship with the victim," Owens said.

"Strictly professional. He was my boss for the last several years between my working in the shop for him when I was in school and in the kitchen once I graduated."

"And was it a good relationship?"

"For much of it. He changed after he got divorced a few years back. Got rather sullen. Unwilling to try new things."

"But you were?"

I nodded.

Owens motioned toward the device. "For the recording, please."

"I was. That was our point of contention the day I got fired." I recounted the conversation we'd had in the kitchen over the lemon curd.

"Explain for us what happened this morning." I did and was immediately asked where I'd been before I went to the bakery.

"Can anyone corroborate where you were?" Owens asked of my answer.

"My cat? He's very chatty." Jay brought a fist up to his mouth to hide his snicker as I continued, "But no. My parents were both asleep in the main house. They said our neighbor Dolores woke them up by calling to say she'd heard the bakery had been broken into."

Owens straightened in his seat. "How did she know that?"

Jay turned to his partner. "A bit of a busybody and the center of our town's gossip."

"What he said," I confirmed. Dolores had kept a watchful eye over my street for years and had called Jay's parents a time or two for things both he and his sister did while we hung out that she didn't approve of.

Voice full of suspicion, Owens asked, "How'd she know about the break-in?"

"She's got a scanner. How else do you think she knows everything that's going on? She's close to eighty now." She wasn't going around killing people, that was for sure.

Owens moved on, although I felt the answer still rankled him. My grandfather had a scanner when I was a kid. My grandmother was always telling him to turn it off, saying it was illegal. It wasn't, but I could understand why someone might not like them. I was pretty sure Dolores's scanner had previously belonged to my grandfather. Picked it up at the estate sale after my grandmother died.

"So am I in trouble for the break-in?" I asked after several more questions from them. "I wouldn't have done it under normal circumstances."

"All things considered," Jay began, "a break-in doesn't compare to a murder investigation, especially when you were trying to check on the victim."

"What my partner means is," Owens continued, "it depends on how the rest of the case plays out."

My eyes widened. "Wait, you really think I could have done something like this?"

Jay started to shake his head, but Owens glared at him. "We'll see what the evidence says. Right now, you have the opportunity and the motive. You've been reported as saying 'You'll regret this' by two witnesses to the argument you and the victim had when you were fired."

I knew I'd regret that statement somehow, but I never imagined it would be for this. My gaze fell to my clasped hands on the table for a moment before I focused back on Owens once more. "That wasn't what I meant, and Stacey and Roni know that. You're taking it out of context. I'd hoped to become the shop manager someday soon, not get myself fired. The business was slowly failing. I was trying to help, but Gio firing me meant I obviously couldn't do that anymore." I turned to Jay. "My blog has a ton of baked goods featured. I always shared with him what I found to be working at other places. He didn't want to listen."

"And you didn't maybe go in early that morning to force him to listen to you?"

I moved my hand in a displaying fashion, palm-up in a downward motion in front of me. "You think I could have taken on Gio? Look at me. I might have baking muscles, but they aren't anything like Gio's."

Owens leaned back as best he could in the wooden chair and crossed his arms. "If not you, then who?"

"I don't know, but it wasn't me. I wish I knew who. I just can't believe he's dead. Murdered. Who would do something like this? It's Wisteria Falls for goodness' sake."

Jay's arm twitched as if he was about to reach out for mine before thinking better of it. "That's what we're trying to get to the bottom of. We won't stop until we find who killed Gio. Mer, if you think of anything that could help us, please let us know."

"Absolutely, I will."

Catching Gio's killer had just become my new job.

Chapter Nine

I'd just reached my car when Jay caught up with me. "Are you okay?"

"Should you be asking a murder suspect that question?" I said glumly without turning to look at him. Instead, I opened my car door.

He softly placed his hand on my shoulder. "Mer, please."

With a sigh, I faced him, hands in my pockets.

The genuine concern in his eyes surprised me. Maybe my mom was right. "Between you and me, you're not a suspect. I remember how excited you were to get to work there. To get into culinary school. How you light up over a delicious blueberry muffin, the kind with the big sugar crystals on top. Even with Gio's attitude change and his firing you, you'd never hurt him. He was practically family."

"Yeah, like a really grumpy uncle," I quipped, but my gaze softened as I watched him standing there, looking at me. I hadn't had a blueberry muffin like that in ages. Gio didn't make them like that. But yet Jay remembered.

Jay chuckled and rubbed the back of his neck with one

hand, highlighting the muscles in his upper arm as it stretched the fabric of his uniform shirt. All the exercising he did to stay in shape for the force had definitely paid off—

And that was enough of that. Mom's comment was getting to me. He'd always been wicked handsome, but I hadn't crushed on him since high school. That was practically half a lifetime ago. And now was *not* the time to start having feelings. A man was dead, and I had to catch his killer. Even if Jay knew I didn't murder Gio, his partner didn't seem too sure.

"Why'd they even let you investigate me, of all people?"

He gave me an incredulous look, and it morphed into one of mock insult as he put a hand to his chest. "Are you saying I'd be biased? You wound me."

"You're my best friend's brother. Known you all my life. Pretty sure you saw me in diapers."

"A lot of people saw the both of us in diapers, Mer. That's just the way the Falls is. Everyone knows you. How would anyone else here be less biased?"

"Your partner doesn't know me. Where'd he come from anyway? How'd I miss someone new coming to town?"

"He came from Boston two weeks ago. Officially my partner last week."

Two weeks ago, I'd been wondering if something was wrong with me because I could hear Trubbs talk, but I couldn't tell Jay that. "Gotcha. I'd only gotten Trouble the week before."

"Bonding time with your new fur baby?"

The corner of my lip curled up at Jay's use of *fur baby*. "Something like that."

He pinched his lips shut to hide his amusement but failed.

"Your sister tell you how I got him?"

He nodded. "Well, Tony did. But I'd like to hear more

about it sometime. From you." He smiled at me in a way that I didn't think he had before.

Was he asking me out? And why was I okay with that if he was?

"I think I'd like to tell you about it, but maybe after we solve Gio's murder? Probably wouldn't look good if one of the cops investigating a case was seen out somewhere with a suspect."

A frown formed on his face. "But I don't think you did it."

"And you're not supposed to be biased. You know how this town talks. I'm sure us just being here in the parking lot is enough for some people." I playfully pushed his arm. "Let's catch Gio's killer and then get a coffee or something. But in that order."

His smile returned. "I'm on it."

"Let me know if you need anything else from me. I'll do whatever I can." Including solving this case. I slid onto the driver's seat of my car.

"Will do. And the same goes for you. Take care of yourself, Mer." He closed my door for me.

Oh my goodness. I kind of had a date. Eventually. With my best friend's brother. What would Rita say? As someone paid to report the news, probably a lot. Both about the potential date and the reason said date was on hold.

I started the engine and put the car in drive. But then a thought struck me. Putting the car back in park, I pressed the button for the window to go down.

"Jay?" He was already several paces away.

Jay turned, his face brightening as he looked at me. "What's up?"

"Is there any way I could get my last paycheck that I'd gone to the bakery for in the first place? It's probably the only money I'll see for a while. Doubt anyone in town will want to hire me right now given the situation." Stacey and Roni would probably be looking for work now too. It would likely be a while before they'd want to step back in the kitchen at Flour Power. That was if it even opened again. Would it with Gio gone?

Jay drew his lips to the side. "I'll go ask. A lot of stuff got bagged as evidence, but I'll see what I can do and give you a call."

"Thanks, Jay." I gave him a wave, then put the car back into drive. The air in the car was warm and stuffy, already cooking in the morning sun, so I left the window open. Maybe the breeze would do me some good.

As I drove away from the station, watching Jay in my side-view mirror wave at me before heading back inside, one thought played in my mind. Who would want Gio dead?

Chapter Ten

As I drove home, that thought stuck with me. I didn't know anyone who disliked Gio enough to kill him. Sure, he was the grumpiest person to ever work with sweets all day, but murder over service without a smile? I didn't think so. But what if it was less about him personally and more about what he had? Without Gio, there was no Flour Power, and without that, there was no bakery in Wisteria Falls. Who had something to gain with it being closed?

Bakeries in the surrounding towns would see a slight uptick in business, but it wasn't enough to kill someone over. They were already pulling business away from us. That was one reason why Flour Power wasn't doing so well, one that tied directly to Gio's refusal to introduce new things to the menu.

Did someone else in town want to start their own bakery enough to get rid of Gio? Possible, but who? Wouldn't that someone already be working at the bakery, getting experience under their belt? One didn't just start a bakery without knowing something about baking. That's how Gio had gotten his start. Gio had been the original owner's right hand. It only made sense for Max to sell to Gio when the time came. The bakery still used some of Max's recipes.

Once upon a time, I'd hoped that would be Gio and me. I'd turn Flour Power into a destination again with my knowledge of travel and tourism. Now? I wasn't so sure if that's what I wanted anymore. Not after everything that had happened.

But what about Stacey and Roni? Did one of them have aspirations I wasn't sure of? Not that I envisioned either one as a killer.

I pulled into the driveway and turned off the car but didn't get out. I'd forgotten to put the volume up on my phone and quickly pulled it out of my bag. Fortunately, Mom hadn't called, but I did have a text.

Clicking on the screen, I smiled softly upon seeing Stacey's name and the message.

Are you okay?

No, she was no killer.

I opened the car door and stepped outside, then quickly waved at my mom in the window. She smiled before letting the curtain fall, no doubt having been checking for me every few minutes. The windows were closed, my parents' AC already running, and I clicked *call* on my phone next to Stacey's name.

It had barely started to ring on my end before Stacey picked up. "Oh my goodness, Mer. Are you okay? What happened?"

"It is so good to hear your voice. I should ask you the same thing. You and Roni both good?"

"Yeah, we're fine. A little shaken. Police met us at the back door to the bakery."

"I'm glad you didn't get inside. No one should have had to

walk in on that." I entered my apartment. Trubbs sat waiting for me on the counter.

"So glad you aren't in jail," he said with a purr. "Can I have a tuna treat?"

Nodding, as I pointed to the phone, I turned to the cabinet where I kept them.

Stacey laughed, the sound making this feel like a normal conversation for a moment. "Your cat hungry or something? I could hear that through the phone."

I opened the cabinet door, then bent down to retrieve the treats. "Or something."

"Milo's a talker, but I don't know if he's ever been that loud."

Over my head, Trubbs jumped from one counter to the next. I usually set the treats down right where he'd landed. Now that he was in the way, I had no room. It wasn't a big kitchen. I spun to the counter behind me, bumping the cabinet closed as I did.

"Hey," Trubbs protested before jumping back across the kitchen. Only this time, he didn't make it as cleanly, and his back paws scrambled up the cabinet to find purchase. I thought he'd make it until he grabbed a stack of napkins with his front paw, losing all grip on the counter. He landed with a thud on the floor. "I better get two after that."

"What was that noise?" Stacey asked.

"Trouble fell off the counter."

She made a humored noise that was sort of like a snort but not quite. Then she sighed. "I can't believe Gio's dead."

"Me neither." I popped open the two cat treat containers. Yes, two. After yet another successful break-in attempt by my unstoppable cat, I'd begun to double seal his treats.

Trubbs ran to his bowl as I put two inside and quickly thanked me before sinking his teeth into the first treat.

"So what happened?" Stacey asked.

"Wish I knew." I grabbed a cup from my drying rack and then filled it with water. I was already on edge this morning, I didn't need to enhance it with a dose of caffeine.

"So you found him, huh?"

I left my kitchen, crossing into the living room. "Yeah. I went to pick up my last check. The door was locked, but the light in the kitchen was on."

"Weird."

"I thought so too," I said, plopping into my chair.

"And the cops?"

I told her about someone reporting my breaking in.

"That must not have looked good. They don't think you did it, do they?"

"I don't know, maybe?"

She scoffed. "That's ridiculous."

"Well . . ." I took a sip of my water. "Two of the people the cops interviewed may have mentioned that I argued with Gio earlier the other day and said he'd regret firing me."

The line was silent a moment. "Oh cr—umb cakes. I wasn't even thinking when they asked us about anything unusual we'd noticed recently. We talked about how he fired you. His best baker. Even though we know you love to travel as much as possible, Roni and I both assumed you'd take over for him someday. I bet even the girls in the shop believed that." The shop girls. I hadn't given them any thought yet. What would they think walking up to the bakery to find it closed this morning, crime scene tape all around?

"I thought I would too. Did anyone call the girls?"

"Roni said she was going to before their shifts started. No sense in having them find out like that. She and I are meeting up again later. You wanna come? Maybe drive out to Neptune

Diner? I've been craving a good lobster roll lately, and they have the best."

I glanced over at Trubbs, who was ambling this way. Maybe he'd like lobster cat treats. "You know? That sounds good. Give me a time, and I'll see you there."

We finished making plans, then got off the phone as Trubbs settled behind me in the chair.

"Can you have lobster?"

He picked up his head. "What is lobster?"

I'd doubted he'd know and had grabbed my computer, explaining that lobster came from the ocean like tuna did and how this part of the Fiddlefern Fjord region was known for them. Once the browser window loaded, I quickly searched for cats and lobster—finding out that it was fine for cats to have in moderation and not as a substitute for their main diet —before pulling up a picture. "This is a lobster."

Trubbs twisted this way and that, then pulled himself up to peek over my shoulder. I grimaced. Cat needed his claws trimmed.

"That is a monster. You eat those?"

"Me? No. I'm allergic. But if you wanted to . . ."

"You expect me to eat *that*?"

"Well, not just like that. I'd turn it into treats for you like I do the tuna."

"Oh, I like treats. Yes. I will eat lobster." Releasing his hold on me, he slid down behind my back once more.

A notification popped up at the corner of my screen. My photos had synched.

What photos?

And then it hit me.

I had taken pictures of the crime scene.

And as much as I didn't want to look at them, I had to.

CHAPTER ELEVEN

I pulled up the images, and it was like I was back in the bakery. Not sure what I was looking for, I looked at everything. Countertops, the stovetops, the floors, and if anything was already in the oven. I avoided glancing at Gio's body the best that I could. For one, I didn't want to remember him that way. And two, I wasn't an investigator and doubted I'd find any clues on him no matter how much I looked. But the bakery and kitchen I knew.

Flour coated the table where dough was sitting out to proof, and the container of flour sat open next to it. Odd. We kept those closed unless using it. Otherwise too much air or moisture would get into it. The dough was there. Made. So Gio had finished what he was doing. Why hadn't he closed the container? That wasn't like him. He would have called that a waste.

But was that a clue? I wasn't sure.

I clicked through the photos again.

There was a lot of flour on that table. There was flour on the floor too. Also a waste. It happened now and again, but that much wasn't something Gio would do. Although this photo showed otherwise. What was going on with him?

"Do you see anything, Trubbs? Maybe something I'm missing or something you saw through the window that I didn't?"

"I'm good at getting in and outta places, not so much the investigating. I wouldn't know what to look for." He yawned.

An email notification popped up on the computer screen.

I clicked into the message, and the police department domain name made my heart leap into my throat. Then I realized it was just a reply to my thank-you message about the candy replacement I'd received, and my blood pressure began to return to normal. I clicked on the email from Grant, the crime scene tech who had helped me a few weeks back the day I got Trubbs.

Glad you got the candy. I hope it's good. I'll be looking for your blog post to find out your thoughts. Thanks again for your help in the case. Turns out your photo was exactly what we needed to point us in the right direction.

Stay out of trouble,

Grant Miller

I thought of the photos in the minimized window. I wondered if he'd see anything I hadn't. It was his job after all.

Worth a shot. I hit reply, then attached the photos I'd taken.

Hi Grant,

Funny you should mention staying out of trouble. Seems it followed me back to Wisteria Falls. Would you mind taking a look at these and letting me know if anything sticks out to you?

I didn't know if I should give him any context or not but decided that less was more in this case. I signed my name at the end and then hit send.

On my drive back from seeing Stacey and Roni at Neptune Diner, my phone rang. I patched it through to my car speakers, a bonus feature when I'd bought the car used from a rental place a few years ago.

"Hello?" I hadn't recognized the number on the dashboard display.

"Is this Meredith?"

The voice was more familiar, though, and I had a good idea who it was. "This is Meredith. Grant?"

"What are you doing with crime scene photos?"

Skipping all pleasantries. "I took them."

"You get a new job in the few weeks since we met? Can't say I was expecting you to leverage your help in the case down here for a career change." The chuckle was evident in his voice.

"I lost a job, actually. The victim was my ex-boss. I found his body this morning when I went to pick up my last check. How are you doing?"

"Oh, wow. Sorry." His tone had changed drastically. "Guess I should be asking you how you're doing."

"I'm okay overall, I guess. But I want to find Gio's killer."

"Don't they have a PD up there?"

"Sure they do. I've already been called in for questioning since they found me with the body."

"You're taking after that cat of yours. He liking his new digs?"

"Seems to, but he won't stay inside."

"Soon you'll be finding dead bodies together. Wait, scratch that. Forget I said it."

"Well . . . he was there with me when I found Gio."

"You brought your cat into a bakery? I mean, I know you got him at a cat café, but Feline Familiar is an exception to the usual."

"He waited outside." Mostly, but Grant didn't need to know that. "He was never in the kitchen where I found Gio. So did you see anything in the photos?"

"The more important thing is did *you* see anything in those photos? Since you worked there, you're the best one to see if something is amiss. At least in the photos you took. Sorry . . . They aren't the greatest."

"I was doing them in a hurry. Before the cops found me."

"You didn't touch anything, did you?"

"Only to check for his pulse." I elaborated on why I didn't think he'd been there long. Then I told him about the flour being open.

"Did you tell them that? That is something only you might know is different."

"I hadn't seen my photos at the time I was questioned. You think they'd let me see theirs?"

"You're not a CSI or detective, Meredith. Tell them what you know about the flour and let them do their jobs."

I turned toward the wharf as I entered town. "Maybe since I'm out of work, I could take your advice and apply for one of these investigator positions."

"That was not advice."

Laughing, I coasted down the hill to the fish market. "I know that. I was kidding. Thank you for calling, Grant. Was there anything else?"

"Wanted to make sure you weren't getting into trouble. It's not every day I get unsolicited crime scene pics in my email. Usually they're just ones I request."

"I'm certainly trying. Thanks for calling."

We hung up as I pulled into the gravel parking lot of the

fish market. The smell of salt air and dried seawater hanging in the humid air enveloped me immediately upon opening the door. The humidity and the salt I was used to. On days when the breeze was strong, I could smell the water no matter where I was in town. It was nice. *This*, however, was overpowering. And the fishy undertones did it no favors. But I'd told Trouble I would get him a lobster, and I couldn't go home without it. This market right on the wharf had the freshest catch around. Only the best for my cat.

In a rush, I didn't take the time to process the familiar car in the lot, but when I approached the counter to pick out my lobster, the scruffy beard, tattoos, and reddish-brown hair were unmistakable. There was no denying who this was.

"Hey," I said, forcing a small smile on my face despite the news I likely had to break. "This is where you ended up?"

CHAPTER TWELVE

"Well, isn't this a surprise." Adam wiped his hands on the cloth draped over his shoulder. "Yes, this is where I ended up. Helps that my dad and brother are out on one of the boats. Started work the next day after what happened. Hours are the same, which is nice. The commute to my job here on the docks isn't bad either. And speaking of work, shouldn't you be at Flour Power?"

I shook my head, not surprised that he hadn't heard about Gio, but slightly taken aback that he'd not heard about me. "Got fired on Monday."

Shock registered on his face as his lips parted. "Oh, wow! I never would have expected that. Me, sure, but you? Nuh-uh. I'm sure the fish market could use some more hands since we're having a busy lobstering season."

"Oh, that's okay, thanks." I'd probably get used to the smell, but I wasn't ready to jump on this lead just yet. "I'm really just here for a lobster . . . and I guess to tell you some other news."

He tipped his head to the side. "What's going on?"

I sighed. "Gio's dead."

Adam's eyes widened, and he staggered a step back. He grabbed onto the whitewashed brick wall next to him. "What? When?"

"This morning. At the bakery." He didn't need to know the details. If he wanted to, he could find out more. No doubt the murder would make the paper come morning, and in a day or two, it would run his obituary too. Did Gio have anyone who could write one since his divorce?

Adam's lips puckered as he blew out a long breath. "Wow. You got any specifics?" When I shook my head, he continued, "Nah, you wouldn't since you got fired. But I'm sorry. Despite whatever happened between you and Gio to get you fired, I know how much you looked up to him. Thought you'd end up running the place someday."

"Me too." But after all this, I wasn't sure what I wanted to do anymore. Struggling to inspire Gio to do something new with the bakery had hurt my motivation. I kept trying, but now that I'd lost my job because of it, was this my sign to try something new? "So how about that lobster?"

"Right," he said, clapping his hands together. "What are you wanting?"

"Doesn't need to be anything special. I'll even take a cull." I wasn't trying to impress Trubbs with my plating, so it didn't matter if the lobster looked perfect from the get-go.

"Pinching pennies now?"

I chuckled. "When aren't I? Though the reason's changed. Don't know how I'm going to afford much travel until I find a new job, never mind finding a place that will give me the time off to do it."

He winked at me. "You got it. We keep those in the back. Hang on." He disappeared through the doorway set into the wall he'd been leaning against since I told him about Gio. A few moments later, he reappeared holding a paper bag, then set it on the scale on the counter. My eyes bulged at the price. Lobster was cheaper on the dock than anywhere else, but how big of a lobster did he get me?

"Don't worry. That's not the cull price. Hang on." He keyed the original price into the register and pressed a button. "Voila!"

"Much better, thanks. My cat thanks you too."

"Your cat?"

"Yeah," I started, digging for my wallet in my bag. "I'm making him cat treats with this."

He laughed. "Now the cull makes sense. That is one lucky cat."

"Let's see if he likes them first. Right now, he thinks they're monsters."

He raised an eyebrow at that.

"Long story." Not that he'd believe me if I told him.

"I'm sure it is." I paid him, and he passed me my change and the lobster bag. "You know how to prep these, right?"

I nodded. I was allergic and couldn't eat them myself, but I'd been to plenty of lobster bakes and boils to know what to do. "All right, guess I should get this guy to my house." I held up the bag.

"It was good to see you despite the circumstances. Guess I'll see you at the funeral if there is one. Gio and I didn't leave off on the best foot, but I'd still like to pay my respects to the guy."

"See you, Adam." I turned and walked back to my car. Popping my trunk to stick the lobster on top of something I didn't mind getting a little damp, a thought occurred to me.

Like Adam had said, he and Gio had not left off on the best foot. Not even on a bad foot. Perhaps the worst. After some quick-witted comments back and forth after Adam showed up late, again, something was said that went too far. Gio at one point had Adam by the collar before he threw him out.

Well, not quite thrown, pushed was more like it.

Gio was all muscle, but so was Adam. Even with Adam not putting up a fight, it couldn't have been easy for Gio to haul him out of the bakery.

I slammed my trunk shut, then scooted to the front of the car and quickly got in as the scene of the two arguing continued to play in my head. Who knows what would have happened if Adam had decided he didn't want to be manhandled by Gio?

I started the car, then backed out of the spot before turning for home.

A startling theory formed in my mind as I drove back to my apartment.

Maybe Adam had stewed over the events leading to his firing and had gone to confront Gio this morning. Only this time when things got heated, Adam wasn't going to let Gio push him around again and took matters into his own hands.

What if Adam killed Gio?

Chapter Thirteen

I wrestled with the thought of one of my friends being a killer as I trudged into the house, lobster bag in hand. No one wanted to think the worst of someone, and being a murderer was one of the worst things I could think of.

But it all made sense.

He knew Gio's schedule as well as anybody. And like me, he would have had to go pick up his last check today. But what I lacked, Adam had. A motive.

That argument inside the bakery had been ugly. The kitchen had remained silent for the rest of the day. Even the girls in the bakeshop had picked up on something being wrong, and we didn't have much interaction outside of them coming in to grab trays to restock cases. The shop was always fully loaded and ready for them to open when they walked in.

Had his reaction to Gio's death been faked? Did he already know about it when I walked in because he had done it?

Trubbs eyed me from the counter as I walked in. "Is it in

there?" His nose twitched as he sniffed the air in my direction.

I nodded, a smirk crossing my face. "You want to look?"

"I think I'll pass. It might make me decide against these treats you're making. Can I have a tuna one?"

"Can't you wait for the ones I'll be making you?"

He flicked his tail. "Even then, I'll still want a tuna one too."

Of that, I had no doubt. His stomach seemed bottomless when it came to his treats.

I set the lobster bag into my empty sink, then opened the cabinet where I kept his treats. Fortunately it was also where I stored my big pot that I needed for the lobster.

Trubbs was sniffing at the bag as I stood with the container of treats, his neck craning as far as it could go as he kept his paws firmly on the countertop. Perhaps feeling a bit braver, he reached out and tapped the bag before pawing the top.

"Sure you don't want to peek?" I asked as I popped the top off the treat container.

Trubbs jumped a foot into the air, landing in the sink and coming much too close for comfort to the lobster inside the bag. He scrambled backward to get out of the sink, making this howling noise that I wasn't sure if only I could hear, and then fell off the counter and onto the floor with a thump. Still not far away enough, he ran behind me.

"I'm not so sure I want monster treats anymore."

"It's a lobster, not a monster. And you can have two of these treats." I pulled two out of the container. As amusing as the sight had been, I felt a little guilty at possibly having caused it by making noise during his intense scrutiny of the bag. But no doubt he'd change his tune by the time the treats were baking in the oven.

He rubbed against my leg as I bent down to feed him. "Thanks."

I scratched the top of his head. "Here you go."

With Trubbs loudly devouring his treats, I set to work getting everything I'd been storing in the pot out. I rarely used it but had been given one because "everyone who cooks in this region should have one." However, I could count the number of times it had been used for lobster on one hand, and one of those times, it wasn't even me using it. I'd let a friend borrow it.

Partway through the pot's cleanout, there was a knock at my door. Stuff surrounded me on the countertop as I tried reorganizing it all to make it easier to put back in once I was done using the pot.

"Come on in," I called.

"What was all that racket?" Mom asked as she poked her head inside.

I laughed. "Trubbs freaked out over the lobster in the sink."

Mom stepped into my apartment, head tilted to the side. "You're making lobster? By yourself? You're allergic."

"It's not for me. I picked one up to make Trubbs some treats." Mom said nothing but gave me a look. Stacking my smaller measuring cup into the larger one, I returned a nearly identical look. I'd inherited it from her. "And before you say it, don't worry. It's a culled one. I wouldn't pay top dollar for one being used for this purpose even with a job. Still, I think Adam may have given me a better price than he should have. That thing is heavy."

She tiptoed around Trubbs and passed behind me on the way to the sink. "Heavy enough that your dad and I could get a little lobster salad?"

"Do you have the stuff for that?" I glanced at the fridge,

trying to envision what I had inside. "I don't think I have mayo. Or celery. But I could bring some plain lobster up when I'm done for you to make it. You know I can't season it to taste anyway."

"Oh sure, sure. I have all that." She peeked inside the bag. "Oh, wow. Definitely a jumbo. Does this Adam fellow like you?"

I barked out a laugh. "Adam? No. He's the baker who got fired the week before I did."

"And he works at the fish market?"

There was something about the way she asked that gave me pause. "He was there behind the counter when I stopped about a half hour ago. Said he's been there since the day after he got fired. Why?"

"You might not remember this because you were away at school at the time, but he was involved in that big wharf brawl several years back. He was banned from the boats."

Adam had a history of getting into tussles, and although I vaguely recalled the incident, I hadn't known of his involvement. But I thought there was a different reason for his not going on the boats anymore. "Really? I thought it was because he got hit in the head on one of their trips and developed motion sickness."

"He got hit, all right. Not surprised someone walked away with repercussions other than concussions." She smiled at her rhyme. "He might get motion sickness, but from what I heard from Dolores, he was also banned from the wharf."

"Technically, the fish market isn't on the wharf. Just really close to it." Only a few feet. I shrugged, unsure of what else to say.

"Still, it's a little surprising for him to be there given how close it puts him in contact with the boats, but they must have worked something out if he was there. His dad and brother probably put their necks on the line for him. Whole family has always done what they can for each other."

"Maybe it's a temporary thing while he looks for other work." Now that it was finally empty, I brought the large pot next to the sink. Mom scooted out of the way for me as I grabbed the spray nozzle to fill the pot without having to put it in the sink and move the lobster. I was sure Trubbs would appreciate it staying put.

"Maybe . . ." Mom said nothing more as I turned on the water, then held the sprayer down to activate it. I doubted that I'd cut her off, but even if I had, I needed the headspace to think. The running water drowned out everything in the background, including Trubbs rattling his dish as he licked it clean of treat crumbs.

Once the pot was full enough for the single lobster, I released the nozzle, sending the water back through the faucet. Carefully, I brought the pot the couple of feet to the stove as Mom turned the water off for me and put the sprayer back in its spot.

We chatted for several minutes more while we waited for the water in the pot to come to a boil, eventually sitting in the living room. Our conversation turned to one of her getting ready to go back to work next week and looking forward to seeing her third graders a couple weeks after that. Mom was a great teacher. And I wasn't just saying that because she was my mom. I had first-hand experience with her classroom skills. She'd also taught me when I was that age.

Finally, the water began to boil. I stood and then headed for the kitchen, Trubbs right behind me. Mom followed but stopped at the end of the counter.

"Well, I'll let you take care of that. My shows are almost on," Mom said as I reached for the lobster. She came up next to me and hugged me from the side. "You want to come up for dinner tonight or just bring the lobster?"

"I think I'll just bring it up tonight."

Mom hugged me once more. "Are you sure you're okay? This morning can't have been easy."

I nodded, tears forming in my eyes at only the reference to what had happened today. Had it only been this morning that I'd found Gio's body? "It's been a long day," I finally said when I knew my voice wouldn't crack.

"All right, well, I'll see you later. Love you."

"Love you too, Mom."

She kissed the side of my head, then stooped to pet Trubbs. He lifted onto his hind legs to meet her hand. "There's a good boy. You take care of her."

Trubbs meowed at her, but I also heard him say, "I will."

Mom chuckled. "It's almost as if he knows what you're saying."

"Trubbs is a smart cat, Mom. He probably does."

Trubbs glanced at me. "Probably?"

That made me smile.

"See? He's doing his job already." Mom stood and then left my apartment.

"Probably?" Trubbs repeated.

"It's not like I could tell her you actually do understand her. That would make me sound like I was losing it. Especially after the day I've had." He flicked his tail. I turned back to the sink and opened the bag with the lobster in it. Wow, it really was a jumbo. I made a show of reaching into the bag, the smile growing on my face. "This is your last chance to look at it if you want."

Before I could turn around, the apartment door closed, opened, and closed once more.

"Trubbs?"

He was gone.

Guess that answered how he was getting in and out of the apartment.

Chapter Fourteen

I went straight from cooking the lobster to prepping the cat treats, setting aside enough meat for my parents to each have a decent-sized lobster roll.

Once I put the treats in the oven, I cleaned up the kitchen. After visiting the fish market and then coming home and working with the lobster, I was ready to get rid of the smell that had followed me home.

Although Trubbs still wasn't back—I doubted he knew how long lobster cooked for—I didn't want to take the chance that he'd come back while I was talking to my mom. He'd end up eating all the treats while they were cooling, then demand I make them all over again. This time without the lobster because I'd already splurged on it once.

As soon as they were cool enough to be dealt with, I wrapped them up and then left my apartment to make my delivery. A cement walkway connected my door at the side of the house to the front door, but the grass in the now hot summer sun felt much better on my feet, so I cut through the yard. It was only as I stepped up onto my parents' landing and knocked on the door that I thought better of dropping this off without at least flip-flops. As I waited for my mom to let me in, I hopped from one foot to the other to keep them from getting too toasty.

Mom opened the door with a chuckle. "Should get flip-flops just for our stairs. You can keep them under the bushes."

I bounced to my right foot before stepping inside with my left. The cool wood floor was much nicer than the stairs. "Trubbs would probably develop a shoe-stealing habit, and then I'd have to stand on the stoop like a flamingo while I waited instead."

"What do you think he is, a dog?"

"Sometimes, I don't know what he is." I certainly hadn't expected a talking cat.

She smiled, having no clue how serious I was, and closed the door as I walked a few more feet inside. "I know we agreed that we'd all knock on each other's doors, but when we're expecting you, you can come right on in."

"And deprive you of this regular entertainment? Never." I held the container out for her, and she grabbed it eagerly.

"Thanks for this. Your father is going to be so excited." She hurried toward the kitchen, and I pivoted to maintain sight of her. "Are you sure you don't want to stay for dinner? We have plenty here aside from the lobster rolls. I could make you a tuna roll . . ."

"Thanks for the offer, but I'm okay. I have some leftovers to finish. Can't let anything go to waste right now."

She nodded in understanding, then opened the fridge. After digging around a moment, she pulled out an armful of supplies.

"Do you want some help?"

The fridge door slammed behind her as she took a step back toward the counter. "If you don't mind."

I hurried over and grabbed the celery and jar of mayo from my mom before it toppled over onto the counter or fell to the floor. "You weren't kidding about having plenty."

"Well, when you said you didn't have mayo to make the salad yourself, I figured I'd head to the store and grab a few things. Maybe put a fun spin on things."

Mom? Putting a spin on things? She never deviated from a recipe. "I never heard you leave."

"And I rarely hear Trouble make any noise when you say he does. Only heard today's racket because of where it was."

She handed me a cutting board, and I grabbed a knife from the block. She always preferred me to chop the celery because my pieces were uniform. I broke two stalks off the bundle and then cut the leafy ends off. "So what is this spin of yours?"

"Well, I thought of making a bruschetta with it—"

"But there's no celery in bruschetta."

"No." She sighed. "I got to thinking about how I *like* my lobster roll recipe. Your father likes it too. So why change it up?"

"What if you liked lobster bruschetta more?"

"But what if we didn't and then didn't enjoy our meal as much? Sometimes it's comfortable to stick with what you know. Risks don't always pan out, and then you could come out with a loss that you can't always get back from. I did buy real lemons to squeeze the juice out of instead of a plastic one, though. Figured that was a safe risk."

I slid the remaining celery stalks back into the bag. "I could make you some bruschetta if you wanted me to."

"Nah, forgot the tomatoes at the store." She chuckled. "Couldn't do it even if I wanted to."

"Mom . . ." I said, drawing out the *ah* sound.

"I know. I was hurrying to get home before my next show

started." She squirted mayo all over the lobster in the container, then dumped it into a large metal bowl before mixing it up by hand.

I added the celery to the bowl. "Can I ask you a question?

"What's on your mind?"

"Who did Adam get into a fight with?" Maybe I could figure out if anything seemed similar to the fight he'd had with Gio and uncover why Adam would want to finish what he started.

She kneaded the celery into the mix. "Some greenhorn. He got kicked off the boats too. Don't know where he headed off to."

There went that idea. "Oh, okay. Thanks."

"So that was your question, now what's on your mind?" I loved my mom, always trying to get at the heart of things. She'd told me once that she realized the questions her students had weren't always what they really wanted to know. So she tried to dig deeper when she got that feeling.

I sighed. "I was thinking about the fight Adam had with Gio."

She handed me one of the lemons. "You think Adam killed Gio?"

"I don't want to, but . . ." Lemon in hand, I shrugged, then rolled the citrus fruit along the countertop to loosen it.

"You said Adam was working, though. They start early at the fish market, don't they? They have to be open for the area's restaurants."

"That's right!" Relief flooded my system, and my shoulders relaxed as I sliced the lemon in half. "He did say that they keep the same hours as the bakery."

"Well, there you have it, then. He was at work and couldn't have done it."

"That does make me feel better, though I don't want to

think that whoever killed Gio is still out there either." I squeezed half the lemon over the bowl, then did the same with the other half. "Who would want to kill him?"

"Wish I could help you there. But don't worry. The cops will find whoever it is. The important thing is they know it isn't you."

I smiled at her, but what she'd said had not made me feel better. "Thanks, Mom. You got the rest of this?"

"Sure do. It's all adding to taste now." She held out her hand, and I passed her the lemon halves. "Thanks for your help."

"Make sure you leave enough for Dad to still have a sandwich." I knew how she could get when things were to taste.

"Hey, that only happened the one time."

I gave her a cheeky grin. "And we will never let you live it down." Before she could say anything else, I scooted to the front door, then shouted, "Love you, Mom!" as I headed back outside.

By the time I'd come back from upstairs, Trubbs was home. His gaze was locked on the cabinet where I'd kept a few treats out so they'd still be warm for him. The rest were in the fridge to stay fresh.

He licked around his mouth. "For something you claimed was so big, there weren't a lot of treats."

"How did you know how many— Wait. Did you eat the ones from the cupboard?" It had only taken a few days for me to need to install a baby lock on the cabinet door to protect his food, but I guess it was no match for him when he was that determined. I'd have to come up with something a bit more secure.

He whipped his head around. "There are more. I knew it!"

"Yes, there are more, but you're not getting them now."

Trubbs walked up to me, his face taking on a look as if I

hadn't fed him in days. Then he begged. "Please . . . they were so good! I like the monster treats. You can bring monsters in whenever you want if it means I can get treats like that."

"You have to wait. Four is more than enough."

"But I want more." He reached up for me with a front paw, tapping my hand before standing to rub his face on my fingers. I gave him a scratch right before he toppled over and landed on the side against my leg. He wasn't the most graceful of cats, but this was a lot even for him. It must have been the catnip baked into the treats. "Oh, you smell like them."

I sniffed at my fingers. I'd washed them a couple times during my kitchen cleanup after finishing the treats. Thankfully they were only a little lemony from helping Mom. Weird that Trubbs would have that reaction. I thought cats hate citrus.

Then I smelled my shirt. He was right, it stunk. I didn't find the scent as appealing as he did, and now that I was no longer nose blind to the smell, I needed a shower. And I'd head to the laundromat afterward for good measure. Wash my kitchen towels and these clothes, not to mention everything I'd been ignoring in the few days since my firing.

I chuckled. No, as nice as Adam's offer was, there was no way I could ever work at the fish market.

Chapter Fifteen

I'd just finished gathering my clothes to take to the laundromat when my phone rang. Wisteria Falls PD flashed on the screen. Crossing my fingers as I pressed *accept*, I hoped Jay was calling about my paycheck.

"Hello?"

"Is this Meredith Duffy?" It wasn't Jay's voice, but I recognized it.

"Officer Owens, how are you? It's Meredith."

"Fine, fine. Look, Miss Duffy, we're hoping that you could help us out with something else regarding the Gio Pinelli case."

"Anything. Name it."

"Could you bring your shoes, bagged, to the station?"

I glanced at the sneakers sitting by the door. "My shoes?"

"Yes. The ones you were wearing this morning when you found Mr. Pinelli. Since you were there, we need to rule out a print we found."

If they wanted to rule me out, that was a good thing,

right? "Sure thing. Let me go find some other shoes to put on, and then I will drive right over."

"Thank you." He hung up. No goodbye or anything of that nature.

Guess laundry would have to wait.

"I'm coming with you," Trubbs said from the top of my clothes pile at the foot of my bed, where he'd been rubbing his face against my shirt from the fish market.

Glancing over my shoulder at the tabby cat, I opened my closet door to look for my other shoes. "Sure you don't want to hang out with my laundry some more? I won't be taking them to wash until tomorrow now."

He flopped over. "Well, in that case."

"I thought so. I'll be home after that. Are you planning on going anywhere?" If he refused to wear a collar and could let himself in and out, the least he could do is tell me when he expected to be home.

Trubbs was on his back now, legs stretched out, belly fully exposed. "Nope, I'm good like this. Only thing better would be another lobster treat."

I chuckled. He thought more with his stomach than anyone else I knew. Then again, I didn't have other cats to compare him to. "Maybe when I get back."

He made a noise, and I couldn't tell whether it was a moan or a groan. Perhaps both.

"Ah ha! There they are," I said as I lifted the lid to one of my suitcases (always a bit of a dumping ground between trips) to reveal my spare shoes. Not bothering to untie them so I wouldn't have to redo the laces, I slipped on my sneakers, said goodbye to Trubbs, then hurried into the kitchen. Under the sink, I grabbed a plastic shopping bag from my box of bags. It used to be fuller. They'd been coming in handy lately since getting Trubbs.

I put my work shoes inside the bag, then tied it closed before heading out of the apartment.

Tony was still at the front desk when I walked into the station.

"Twice in one day, Mer. Rita's going to get jealous."

"Have you talked to her at all today? About what's going on, I mean."

"Are you asking if I've told my news reporter wife about the first murder in town in nearly two decades? Oh, she knows." He glanced at the clock. "You just missed her, actually. She's probably getting ready to film a segment for tonight's news in front of the bakery."

Although I was well aware of what my best friend did for a living, I hadn't even thought about how word of Gio's murder would spread beyond Wisteria Falls. Rita worked for the regional station. Everyone within at least an hour and a half's radius would know what happened, and soon.

"Rita's thrilled, actually," Tony continued. "Not about Gio, of course, but that she can cover a story like this and get the scoop on everyone. You know both her brother and I promised that we'd only talk to her if something big ever happened here."

I chuckled. "You even made it a part of your wedding vows."

"Course I did. It was wicked important to her. Didn't expect anything to happen here, though. Our big news is more like that cow escaping the truck and roaming the streets before getting lost in the woods."

The footage of the cow walking down Main Street had gone viral online earlier this summer. Had given my blog a good boost in traffic for a week or so after I posted a walking tour of the cow's path the day after it happened. It was still one of my top-viewed posts. "Anyone ever find him?"

Tony shook his head. "He's gotta turn up eventually."

I pursed my lips to the side. "Does Rita know that I'm involved?"

"Not that you found him. You know we can't give her that sort of information"—he leaned forward on the desk—"but don't be surprised if she wants an interview as one of his former employees."

I looked down at my outfit. Thank goodness I'd showered. No doubt she'd come looking for me soon. She had easy access to cover multiple angles of this case between me and the police. This was huge for her, and if it could help shed light on Gio's murder and maybe give Jay some new leads, then I was all for it. With Adam being ruled out (at least by me) because he had been at work, there was no one else to investigate that I could think of.

"So what are you back here for?" Tony asked, drawing me away from my thoughts.

"I'm looking for Jay or his partner." I held up the bag. "They wanted my shoes."

He nodded as if that made all the sense in the world and then picked up the phone with one hand while pressing a button on the cradle with the other. "Meredith Duffy is here . . . Thanks." He turned back to me. "Owens will be right out."

I must have made a face. All I knew was my nose had twitched, and I tried to cover it by wiping a loose fist under my nose.

Tony stifled a chuckle. "Aww, he's not all that bad. A little rough around the edges, but he'll loosen up. He's never worked in a small town before."

"I hope so for Jay's sake. Owens considered me a suspect in this. *Me*."

At that moment, someone cleared their throat behind me.

"Everyone's a suspect until we can rule them out." I stiffened at Owens's comment. I hadn't heard him walk in. "And hopefully, that's what we can do with your shoes, Miss Duffy."

I held the bag out, practically shoving it at him. "Here you go."

"If you don't mind." He turned and waved me forward from over his shoulder, half pointing down the hall.

He hadn't taken my shoes, and I deflated slightly. I just wanted it over. But wanting to be as helpful as I could now that he'd confirmed I was a suspect until I could be ruled out, I followed him back to the room I'd been in earlier.

Jay was already there, a manilla folder in front of him, and he smiled upon seeing me, easing some of my tension. "Mer, good to see you again. Thanks for coming back down. This shouldn't take long." He motioned to the chair I'd sat in this morning, and I walked over to it.

"Like I told Officer Owens on the phone, anything I can do to help."

Officer Owens closed the door behind us and headed for his earlier spot. "I'll take the shoes now, thanks."

I pushed them across the table as Jay uncapped the marker and wrote something on the empty bag. I'd seen bags like this before, mostly on TV but recently in person on the return trip from Saltair Shores, where a man had died on the tour bus we'd been on.

Jay capped the marker, placed it back on the table, and then lifted the large evidence bag now marked with my name, the date, and some numbers that I assumed were related to the case.

Owens unknotted the bag with my shoes and peeked inside before dumping them into the evidence bag.

"Am I going to get those back? They weren't cheap." Between all the standing on my feet I did at the bakery and all the walking when I traveled, I did not skimp on footwear. I learned that lesson in college when my tourism class went on a walking tour in the rain. My cheap shoes were soaked through and resulted in blisters for days. It made working in my kitchen lab classes tough that week.

"If everything checks out and you aren't guilty, yes, you will get them back."

"Okay. Last time I submitted evidence, I had to get a replacement."

Officer Owens raised an eyebrow.

I held up a hand. "It was food and unrecoverable. And no, I was not a suspect in anything. They offered me replacements since I'd bought the candy to taste test for my blog."

Owens nodded slowly, his face pinched as if he were questioning something, perhaps his decision to come up to Wisteria Falls.

"And it all worked out," I continued. "That's how I got my cat."

He perked up at that. "You have a cat?"

"I do. His name is Trouble. He was waiting outside the bakery for me this morning, remember?"

Jay made an amused-sounding noise with his throat, but Owens grew serious.

"We were going to go to the pet store after I picked up my paycheck," I added. We still had to go, but we couldn't do that without being paid first.

Owens pulled the folder from in front of his partner and flipped through the papers and photos inside. He stopped on a sheet of text, then leaned toward Jay and mumbled something.

Jay's smile slipped. "Mer, did Gio have a cat?"

"Not anymore, I don't think. He used to. Before the

divorce. He was wicked strict about cat fur on our clothes. He yelled at me about it a couple times."

"Your cat, Trouble, he's got short fur, yes?" Owens asked, flipping through to what I could tell was a picture, my view obscured by the pages above it.

"Yes. White, silvery-gray, and black. Tabby. Why?"

"Doesn't match." Jay sighed, then clarified with a worried tone in his voice. "Not that I thought it would. But it's another unknown."

I smiled at him to let him know I understood as I thought about who else had cats. Stacey had Milo, but she was meticulous about the lint roller. If she was Gio's murderer—and she wasn't—she wouldn't have left cat fur behind. Roni had a dog, and although she was good friends with Stacey (enough for the occasional strand of cat fur to be on her), there would have been dog fur on Gio, too, had it been her.

"Trubbs will be glad to find out he doesn't have to submit a fur sample." If not Stacey or Roni, did any of the girls from the shop have cats? But it was too early for them to have been there, and besides that, I doubted they were killers.

Jay laughed once more as Owens clarified, "It's not like he'd have to come to us. You could just get the fur from him as one of us watched. Chain of custody reasons."

I nodded slowly. "In that case, is there anything else you need me for, or were the shoes it?" I didn't see why I needed to be back here if all I had to do was hand over the shoes. How were they any different from what Owens said I could do with Trouble's fur?

"There is one more thing," Jay said hesitantly, "but I'm not sure if you're going to like it."

Chapter Sixteen

O wens made a huffing sort of noise, suggesting he didn't like whatever it was either. Interesting . . .

Jay glanced at his partner. "Come on. Mer's no killer. It's not like you or I have ever worked in a bakery."

"Fine." Owens looked up at the ceiling in a near eye roll.

"What is it, Jay, I mean, Officer Roland?"

"Could you look at these? They're crime scene photos. Both inside the bakery and the kitchen. You know the space probably better than anyone."

I straightened. "Just the spaces?"

He nodded with a kind, sympathetic smile. "I wouldn't ask you to do more."

"Okay." I unclasped my hands, and Jay removed a stack of photos from the folder, then slid them toward me. It was then I remembered the flour in the photos I'd taken. Probably a little too late to say I had taken photos as well. Not that they would show anything different.

I pored over these, which for obvious reasons had been taken at much better angles and got closer to things than I had been able to from where I was standing. The only thing that stood out was the flour, but one area was missing.

"The footprint was in the flour, wasn't it?"

"How'd you know?" Owens asked.

"There's no picture directly below this counter, and with the amount of flour here, there has to be flour on the floor." They didn't need to know I already knew it to be true.

Owens nodded in short slow strokes, his chin jutting out slowly. "Impressive."

Jay turned to his partner. "That might be the first nice thing you've said to her."

Glaring at him, Owens's mouth tightened into a hard line, and one eye squinted more than the other.

Ignoring the look, Jay asked me, "What are you thinking?"

"It's a lot of flour. The bread is already proofing." I pointed to the open container of flour that I'd seen in my photos. "And this would usually be closed."

"Could he have been starting something?"

I shook my head. "It's too much flour, officer. More than is needed to prep a surface. If he was making something, you'd see the bowl it was going into. The measuring cups. Gio could eyeball an amount pretty accurately, but baking is a science, you can't just grab a handful of flour and hope it's enough when something requires an exact amount." Seeing it from this angle, there was something else about the flour that bugged me, but I couldn't put my finger on it.

"What if he was caught by surprise?

I pulled a face. It wasn't a possibility I'd considered until then. Finally I shrugged. "Maybe? I don't know. I'm sorry. That could explain why the container wasn't closed. If he didn't have the time to put it back on before . . ."

Jay reached out and placed a hand on my arm. I was pretty sure he wasn't supposed to do that with anyone they were questioning. Was I even being questioned now? Or had his request for me to look at photos morphed into me helping them?

"If you need a minute, we'd understand."

Owens coughed, and Jay removed his hand, but not before he gently squeezed my forearm.

"I'm okay. Really." As strange as it was, that was the truth. "But it still feels so surreal."

"Do you need a drink or anything?" Jay asked, concern in his eyes.

I shook my head and flipped to the next picture in the stack. "Let's just get through the rest of these photos."

Finally, after twenty and forever minutes, I'd finished going through the photos. I doubted I'd ever scrutinized photos so heavily, not even the selfies I took for my blog of me eating food, and I always took a lot of those to make sure I didn't look weird.

"That's it. There's nothing else. Outside of the flour—and what happened, obviously—it looks like a normal early morning in the bakery." I sighed hard. "I'm sorry I can't be of more help."

Jay reached out again but stopped short of touching my hand. Instead, he hesitated a moment and took the photos from me. "This is a huge help. We may have overlooked something like that. Thank you. Really." He gave me an encouraging smile.

"I hope it's enough."

Owens cleared his throat. "Thanks for coming in, Miss Duffy. If we have anything else, we'll let you know."

They might have been done with me, but I wasn't done with them.

"Any news on whether I could get my paycheck? I really do need the money. Trubbs needs cat food and a harness."

Owens's eyebrow shot up. It seemed like he wanted to say something, and his lips parted slightly, but ultimately, he remained silent.

Jay nodded. "We kept the envelopes as evidence to check for prints, but it was determined that you all could have the contents inside them, as the envelopes were sealed." He flipped through several more things in the folder before stopping and pulling a familiar paper out of it.

"Thank goodness. And thank you for this. I bet the girls will be glad they can get their checks. Adam too."

"Adam?"

"Yeah. Adam Chambers. Works over at the fish market now. He got fired the week before me. Would have been his last check too."

Owens pulled the folder from Jay and opened it up to where I could see another pay slip. He flipped through two more pages, then went to a page higher in the stack.

Jay leaned toward Owens, mumbling something, and the two turned away from me, making it even harder to hear.

Craning my neck to try to pick up on their conversation to no avail, I finally asked, "What is it?"

Jay turned back to me. "There was no check for Adam at the bakery."

Owens's annoyance shined through his glare at Jay's admission, but the news left me confused.

"There had to be a check for him. He wouldn't have had another opportunity to get it."

"Unless he was the killer," Owens commented.

"Not possible. I talked to him. He was at work."

Owens furrowed his brow. "What are you doing investigating?"

In the span of several hours, I'd gone from suspect to investigator in his mind, and his tone said my looking into the case was unwanted, even though my running into Adam had been completely accidental.

"I had no idea he'd be at the fish market." Resisting the urge to cross my arms, I recounted my conversation with my former coworker.

"Thank you for telling us." Owens actually seemed grateful for the new information. "We'll look into it."

"And hey," Jay said, his tone hopeful. "If we determine he was at work, then he can't be the killer. There are other ways people can get checks."

I shook my head. "Gio never switched to direct deposit." It was one more thing he didn't want to change about how he ran the bakery.

"We'll look into it," Owens repeated as he pointed at me. "You stay out of it."

"I agree with him on this, Mer. It's a murder investigation. We don't know who killed Gio or why. Please stay safe."

"You think this could go beyond Gio?"

"Mer, please. We really don't know. Can't you try to stay safe just in case?"

"Okay, okay. I won't do anything dangerous. Don't worry."

It was the closest I could come to saying I would stay out of it without becoming a liar, because I couldn't lie. Not to Jay.

I *was* going to investigate.

I'd just have to hope I could stay safe while doing it.

Chapter Seventeen

Check in hand, I was ready to grab Trubbs and take him for a late run to the pet store. Today's events had been far from usual, and I was looking forward to doing something that resembled normalcy. Or what would become normal for us. After all, how many people took their cat shopping? Dogs, yes. I'd even seen a teacup pig once. But cats?

Although I'd discovered several cats like this on social media while working on my blog's rebranding, I personally didn't know any who took kindly to being walked around on a leash or staying still when told, but Trubbs had agreed he'd listen if it meant I would take him places. Thank goodness Trubbs was no ordinary cat. He wouldn't have been even if he couldn't talk, but in our case, it helped.

The lobby was noisy and grew louder as Jay led me back to the front of the station.

"Thanks again for your help," Jay began. "And I'm serious about what I said about you keeping safe."

I was about to respond when I saw the crowd at the front

desk and instead glanced up at Jay and asked, "What's going on?

He looked forward and stopped, grabbing my arm to halt my step. "Reporters. Probably about Gio."

"I thought Rita was on top of it."

"Oh, she is. That doesn't stop others from trying. In fact, there she is." He made a short motion with his head, and when I looked back toward the crowd, I spotted my best friend standing at the front, a slightly confused look on her face.

I smiled at her, and she raised her eyebrow at me, or us. Jay let go of me, and a smirk flashed on Rita's face. One I remembered well from high school as she tried to dig for gossip about our crushes. Maybe my mom had been right.

"Might I suggest the side entrance to the lot so you can avoid all of that?" Jay suggested.

"But they don't know—"

"I meant my sister. If she talks to you now, the rest will follow."

"Oh. Got it."

"I'm sure she'll figure it out and come find you." He pivoted on his heels, then directed me through a different doorway. "We'll cut through here."

I followed him through the dispatch office, waving at Nancy at her desk in dispatch as we passed, and then down another short hallway with lockers before coming out at a third hallway running along the side of the building. The windows were small, and there was only one door.

He pointed. "That will get you right to the parking lot. Just head through the gate to get past our lot and into yours."

I took a step, then paused. "Am I allowed to be doing this?"

"Probably not, but I don't want you to get stuck talking to

a lot of reporters either. Only my sister." He let out a short chuckle.

"Thanks, Jay. You didn't have to do this."

"And let my little sister miss out on her exclusive scoop with her best friend? No way. You take care of yourself, Mer."

"You too. I hope you find whoever did this soon. Thanks for my check."

"I hope so too, and you're welcome. I'll let you know about your shoes as soon as I hear from forensics."

"Thanks." With my hand on the door, I glanced back with a smile. "See you around."

I wasn't surprised to see Rita already at my car waiting for me, although how she was hunched down on the passenger side was quite a sight.

"Are you hiding?" I asked with a laugh.

She looked at me but didn't stand fully. "I didn't want the others to see where I'd gone. I even sent the van with my driver ahead of me. You are my exclusive . . . at least until tomorrow."

"Why tomorrow?"

"They'll know your name after that and be able to find where you live. But there are other former employees they could talk to first, but none knew him as well as you did."

No one else had found his body either, but she didn't know that yet. Jay hadn't told me not to tell her, but if that got out everywhere, no doubt it would cast the town's eyes on me. One more reason to find Gio's actual killer.

"Why didn't you get in the car?" She knew me well enough to know the doors were unlocked.

"Why didn't you roll down your windows? It's a hot day."

I popped my door open, then leaned in to turn on the car and get the windows down. I didn't want to be in the hot car either. Rita opened the passenger door and put the AC on blast to get that started too. Then she walked around to the back of my car.

"A lot on my mind today," I finally answered when I met her at the trunk.

She pulled me in for a hug. "Sorry about Gio."

"It's just so weird. Who would want him dead? Have you gotten any leads yet? Who have you talked to?"

She shook her head. "His neighbors, several shop owners near the bakery, my mom, Naomi—"

"How's she doing?" Even though they'd been divorced a few years now, I couldn't imagine that she'd taken the news well.

"About as you'd expect. It's a shock. A shock to everyone, really."

"You're telling me." I'd have to bring Naomi flowers. I'd always liked her.

Rita placed her hand on my arm. "How are you?"

I shrugged. "Okay, I think." The car made a noise, and I turned. It probably wasn't happy sitting like this. "Come on. Where do we need to go?"

She walked back to her side of the car, and we both got in. It had cooled significantly inside, although the air was still blowing warm and would until we got moving.

"I told the crew to meet me in the park. If anyone else wants to know where you live, they're going to have to do some legwork. I'm not going to roll up to your house and make it easy for them." She smiled.

"Smart. And thank you." I put the car into drive, and we headed out of the parking lot, the other reporters and news crews none the wiser. "I'm sure my parents appreciate it, if for nothing more than they won't have to deal with Dolores's phone calls asking about what's going on."

"She's so nosey."

"She means well." That was easier to say now that she wasn't letting my parents know that I'd broken curfew or snuck out of the house—usually with Rita. "Called my parents this morning and woke them up to tell them something was happening at the bakery."

"This may have convinced me to get a scanner."

I cracked a smile. "The runaway cow wasn't enough?"

She snorted. "No. That's funny, but it's not what makes someone's career."

"Murder does, though."

Her eyes lit up, no doubt at the thought of scooping everyone that much earlier. But I had a hard time faking my excitement for her. Maybe if it hadn't been Gio and I hadn't found him.

"Yeah," she cleared her throat, her demeanor dimming slightly and taking on an air of concern. "Is that how you found out? Your parents? How's the job hunt?"

"Stalled right now. Kinda waiting to see what happens with all of this. Job hunting doesn't feel right."

She nodded slowly. "You avoided my first two questions."

"You're meant for this investigative reporter stuff, you know. My parents are fine. And to answer your first question, no. It wasn't." I pulled into the parking lot of the local park. It wasn't too crowded at the moment. The heat had probably chased people away. "On the record or off? I don't know if I'm supposed to tell." Though Jay said he couldn't tell her, he hadn't told me that I couldn't.

Rita unbuckled her belt and shifted to face me. "Off. We're still in the car. What's going on?"

"I found Gio this morning. I was there to pick up my last check."

Suddenly I found myself with arms wrapped around me.

"Oh my goodness! Mer, I'm so sorry! I can't imagine how

awful that must have been." She went quiet a moment before holding me out at arm's length. "Are you the one who broke into the bakery too?"

"How'd you know about that?"

"I may not have a scanner, but I saw the police log. Are you in trouble for that?"

I shook my head. "Not yet anyway. Gio's murder is more important."

"Right. So that explains why you were with my brother, then. I wasn't sure if you had a lead or something."

"Wish I did." I explained to her about the shoes. "That's probably something they don't want getting out either so the killer won't toss evidence."

She made a zipping her lips motion, then looked out the window before waving to a man holding a camera. "I won't say a word, but we should probably get out there and get you on camera saying something. We can just pull the former employee card. No one needs to know anything."

I let out a long breath. "Okay. I can do that."

"And then I'm coming over once I submit my report and film my spiel. We'll get pizza and ice cream, my treat." A knowing smile spread across her face, and in a semi-teasing voice, she added, "And then you can talk to me about what's going on with my brother. I saw his hand on your arm as he guided you out of the police station."

Now *that* I wasn't sure I could do.

Chapter Eighteen

A girls' night with Rita was exactly what I needed to end my crazy day. It had been too long since she and I had done one of these.

Trubbs wasn't initially thrilled that I was having someone over, but when I told him it meant I'd be delaying doing my laundry until morning, he was all for it. Seemed my smelly "monster" clothes had become his new favorite spot.

And then once Rita started giving him cat treats, more than he should have had—but he was playing up being nervous around her to keep getting them (not that I could tell her how I knew that)—he was thrilled with the concept of girls' night.

"When is she coming back over?" he asked as soon as Rita left.

"Soon, I hope, Bubba."

"You don't get to call me that. Only Rita does."

I snickered. I'd let that be their pet name. "Okay. What if I give you as many lobster treats as she did?"

"Then maybe." He squinted at me. "Are you going to give me more treats?"

"Sure," I replied before heading to the cupboard to get a glass for water. "Over the next few days."

Trubbs jumped up on the counter next to the sink, then gave the empty basin a quick glance before turning back to me. "Not cool, Meredith. Not cool."

"What's not cool is the tummy ache you'd end up with if you have any more today." I filled up my cup, then refreshed Trubbs' water. He hadn't touched his dinner, but given what he'd been eating instead, I couldn't blame him.

He followed me as I walked to my bedroom, and by the time I had fallen asleep after gathering all of my clothes to take to the laundromat in the morning, he'd settled into his usual spot wrapped around my head at the top of my pillow against my headboard.

Trubbs was gone when I woke up, but that was nothing to be concerned about. He'd routinely take off first thing. During our first week together, before I got fired, that meant him leaving when I did. This week it had meant he left while I sat with an extra cup of coffee since I wasn't grabbing one on the way to work. Yesterday had been the exception, but he'd wanted to be there for me as I picked up my check.

After a quick shower—Trubbs liked to suck on my hair, and it was not a good morning look, even to do laundry—I got dressed and then grabbed my hamper. Hopefully the place wouldn't be too busy this early on a Saturday morning because, didn't people like to sleep in on weekends? I did once. Working at the bakery and my travel bug had changed that.

There were a few cars in the lot as I pulled in, and the door to the laundromat was wide open, making it easy for me to carry all my laundry inside. Who knew how heavy it could get when you let it all pile up? Right, I did. I'd been guilty of doing this since college. No one wanted to lug their laundry down four flights of stairs and back more than was necessary, but it made each trip that much heavier.

I trudged over to the closest open machine, nodding at Paula, the woman behind the counter as I passed her.

She gave me a sympathetic smile, then said, "Saw you on the news last night. Sorry about Gio. What's going to happen to the bakery?"

Heads turned in my direction as the other two women in the laundromat waited for my answer.

"No idea." I picked up the bottle of detergent I had in the hamper, then set it down on the washing machine. Although I doubted it would be me now, I hoped someone would take over Flour Power eventually. Even if it got a new name, the town needed a bakery, and although Gio wasn't doing much with it, the spot on Main Street was a great place to have one.

I opened the door to the washing machine, then reached down to grab my first armful of laundry.

Something was very wrong.

The laundry moved in my arms, but I was already in the motion of tossing it into the circular opening of the machine.

"Oh my goodness!" I cried at the same time Trubbs let out a yowl I'd never heard him make before.

"What's going on?" he yelled as he scrambled out of one of my shirts. He jumped unceremoniously into my hamper and tipped it over, scattering my clothes and trapping himself under the overturned plastic basket.

"Trouble! I'm so sorry." By now, everyone was looking at us again, this time with even more interest than they had when waiting for my answer about the bakery.

"Is that a cat?" Paula asked.

Gathering up the clothes that had spilled out of the

hamper and throwing them into the wash, I said, "I had no idea he was in my laundry. I'm so sorry."

"I want to go home," he wailed. "Let me out of here."

"Is it all right if I get these started and then come back?" I'd never left before, always choosing to sit there and use the time to read or work on my blog.

Trubbs let out a pitiful sound as Paula answered, "Of course. Plenty of people do."

"I can find my way home," Trubbs said, poking his front paw through one of the holes in the basket. "Let me out of here."

"I can't just let you go home from here on your own. They don't know you like I do," I whispered. "Cats don't usually do that."

"Get me out of here." He stretched his arm through the hole as far as it would go.

"You can't go running off."

"I make no promises."

"I'll give you a treat when we get home." Hopefully I could appeal to his stomach if I couldn't appeal to his head.

Trubbs squinted, weighing the deal. "Two."

I grabbed his paw and shook. "Deal."

He pulled it away and back through the hole. "But let me out of this thing. I'll go wait by the car until you're done. This is embarrassing."

"Fine." I lifted the hamper off Trubbs, and he shot out from under the basket and rushed out the door.

"Oh no!" one woman over by the dryers gasped.

"Shouldn't you go after him?" Paula asked.

I glanced out the window. He was on the roof of my car, licking his paw and then bringing it up to wash his ear.

"No, I think he'll be fine. He's already pretending it didn't happen."

The people in the laundromat all turned to the window as I pointed, and stared at Trubbs.

"That is quite the cat," one commented.

"Mine would never have done that. Would have taken off running," said another.

I laughed off the comments. "Yeah, he's something, isn't he? Wicked smart."

A few minutes later, my laundry was in the machine, the hamper on top of it claiming my spot, and I was back at the car. As Paula watched, I opened the car door for Trubbs, and he hopped right inside.

Once I was in my seat, with door closed and belt on, I apologized to him again. "I had no idea you were in there. Thought you'd left like you usually do in the mornings. You didn't say anything the entire time I was getting ready."

"I was asleep," he grumbled.

I backed out of my spot and headed for home. "Next time, I'll check. I promise."

"I would certainly hope so."

By the time he'd finished his first treat, Trubbs and I were back on solid footing. I knew it wouldn't take long. He seemed to like these more than the tuna ones, but I hoped he realized these were special occasion treats. I couldn't afford the lobster all the time. At least with the tuna ones, I could wait until a sale on the cans and make myself some tuna salad for sandwiches as well. But as he sat happily munching on the second treat, I didn't have the heart to remind him of that fact. He had another four treats, and then it would be time to break the news to him.

I left the house to go back to the laundromat as he was

finishing the second treat. My clothes still had a few more minutes in the wash, so I plopped into the chair across from the machine and grabbed my phone. Not wanting to get into anything with the wash finishing soon, I surfed the web until the buzzer sounded, then carted my wet laundry across the building to the dryers in the back.

I was just about to settle into my ebook when a folded newspaper with Gio's face in black and white appeared in my line of vision.

"Thought you might like to see this about Gio if you haven't," Paula said.

"Thank you. I hadn't yet." I took the copy of our local paper, the *Vine*, from her outstretched hand.

"Murder made the front page. No surprise there. Such a shame. I'm going to miss those blueberry muffins."

"They were some of my favorites." To eat and make. Maybe I was going to miss working at the bakery more than I thought I would.

Paula gave me a small smile before turning away to greet the woman who had just walked in. I recognized her from town, as I did most everyone, but I didn't know her name.

"Missed you yesterday morning," Paula said as she walked back toward the counter.

"Ugh, yeah. Had to cover part of a shift for the new kid. Just started at the market not even two weeks ago and already asking for time off. Now I gotta deal with all these fishy clothes on my day off instead."

Paula shook her head. "Craig must have a lot of pull to get his boy a job after what happened."

I peeked over the newspaper that I had yet to start reading. My interest had been piqued at the mention of the market and the fish smell, but hearing Craig's name clinched it.

"Are you talking about Adam?" I asked when the woman whose name I didn't know was close enough.

"Yeah, why?"

"I was at the fish market yesterday getting lobster, and he'd said he'd been there all morning."

She scoffed and rolled her eyes. "If you count all morning as coming in at eight thirty when he's supposed to be there at five."

A lump formed in my throat, and I swallowed it down. "That rots," I told the woman.

"Like a stinky fish." She chuckled at her joke.

I couldn't really clue her into the fact she'd just poked a huge hole in Adam's alibi, but I had to tell Jay what I'd heard.

This meant Adam had the opportunity to go to the bakery, confront Gio, kill him, take his paycheck, and even deposit it before going to work. He probably had time to go home and shower to destroy any evidence too. He used to talk about how quickly he could get ready in the morning before work, needing only ten minutes between getting up and heading to work. I doubted that routine had changed.

Setting the paper down, I pulled my phone back out and scrolled through my contacts to find Jay's number. I probably should have called the station, but I wasn't guaranteed to get Jay if I mentioned it was about Gio's murder. I did not want to talk to Owens and get accused of investigating again.

So instead, I shot Jay a quick text saying to call me.

Chapter Nineteen

It wasn't until I was out of the laundromat and back in my car that my phone finally rang.

"What's going on, Mer?" he asked as soon as I finished saying hello, his voice filling my car.

"Jay, have you talked to Adam yet?"

"We called him, but we're following up on another lead at the moment, why?"

"He wasn't at work when he said he was."

"How do you know that? What did I say about staying out of it?" Unlike his partner's, Jay's voice held concern instead of annoyance at my being involved in the case once again.

"I wasn't trying to be in it. Honest. I was doing my laundry." I told him what I heard from the woman who'd covered part of his shift at the fish market, staying in the car even after I'd pulled into the driveway at home so I could say everything without anyone overhearing.

There was a brief pause, and the line went completely silent. I thought the connection had dropped, but when I checked it, my phone screen said otherwise.

"Mer, you still there?" Jay finally asked. He must have muted me.

"Are you going to look into it?"

"Of course we are."

"But you have your other lead." Maybe this would all turn out to be nothing. "What is it?"

"You know I can't tell you that. But hey, while I have you on the phone. How's your job hunt?"

He couldn't talk to me about Adam because of this new lead, but he had time to ask me how that was going?

"I've not even thought about it since before yesterday morning."

"Think you could go help my mom out at the shop? Like we suspected, she's swamped with orders because of Gio's funeral tomorrow."

"That's tomorrow? Fast." I should have taken the time to look at the article in the paper while I was at the laundromat, but I'd been too busy checking my phone to see if I'd somehow missed Jay's call and trying to hear anything else the woman from the fish market was saying. What if she had unknowingly provided me with more information about Gio's murder?

"Yeah. Anyway, she could use the help."

"I'll stop in as soon as I drop my clothes off at the house. I was going to take Trubbs to the pet store since we didn't get to go yesterday, but I'm sure he'll understand."

He chuckled. "I heard my sister named him Bubba."

"Yeah, but don't you go trying to call him that. That's a name just between them."

This time, a burst of laughter bubbled out of him. "Oh? Is that what he told you?"

Yes, but I wasn't going to admit that. "No, but you should have seen the look he gave me when I tried to use it. Guess

I'm sticking to Trouble or Trubbs. You'll have to figure out what to call him sometime." Did that just come out of my mouth?

"I'd like that." Yes, I had, and then he agreed. Oh my goodness. He really did like me. I hadn't wanted to fully believe Rita last night when she confirmed it, asking me where I'd been this whole time to not realize it.

"Well, once we solve Gio's murder, you should meet him."

"Yes, when *we* solve the murder. Owens and I."

"That's what I meant."

I could sense the rise of his eyebrow through the phone. "It's not what you said. Please, Mer."

I needed to get off the phone before making a promise I couldn't keep. "So I'm at my house, and I'm going to let you go."

"How come I have a feeling you're purposely not agreeing?" He sighed. "Have a good day, and thanks for helping my mom."

"Sure thing. You take care. Bye, Jay." We hung up, the car's silence seeming louder than it usually would. I pulled my phone out of its holder on the dash, tossed it in my bag, and then got out of the car.

As I carried my laundry into the house, I couldn't help but notice how much lighter it was than earlier. Poor Trubbs. I should have picked up on it being heavier than it was supposed to be. Oh well, at least I'd be more careful from now on. And hopefully, so would he.

"Trubbs, you here?" I called as I walked into the apartment. Although I hadn't heard a response (able to talk or not, he was still a cat and was thus good at ignoring me), I continued, "You will not believe what I heard from the lady from the fish market."

He launched himself into the hamper from somewhere

above me. Maybe the refrigerator? The force of his landing shot the hamper out of my hands, and it landed with a loud thump on the floor in front of my feet.

Trubbs seemed unperturbed. "Fish market? Does that mean you brought me home more monster, I mean, lobster?"

"Sorry, no. I didn't *go* to the fish market. One of the women I saw at the laundromat works there."

"Oh," he said flatly, turning and high stepping out of the hamper. "Well, what did you hear?"

I brought my clothes into the room as I recounted the conversation.

"So your source for cheap lobster might be the killer again?"

Folding a pair of pants, I sighed hard. "Yeah. I don't want to think it, but he lied to me about where he was."

"I don't want to think it either. His being guilty means fewer treats for me. So if he didn't do it, I want to help prove it. Consider me officially on the case."

I pressed one hand against my chest. "Who said *I* was even on the case?"

He squinted at me. "Pretty sure you did. You called it your new job."

"Oh shoot!" I dropped the shirt I was about to fold back into the hamper.

Trubbs sat at attention. "What?"

"I said I'd go help Mrs. Roland at her store." I turned and looked at myself in the mirror. Jeans and a plain fitted t-shirt. "Think this is okay to wear at a florist? Maybe I should change my pants." I opened my drawer and plopped the pants I'd already folded inside it, then dug around for a pair of khakis. That seemed like a safe option, and I didn't want to wear any of my black pants. Putting one on right now would feel too much like I was getting ready for the bakery.

"Do you know what you'll be doing?"

"No. I don't have a lot of experience with flowers. Well, sugar ones, I do."

"Then you'll be fine."

"Does it matter if she's also Rita and Jay's mom?"

"Oh . . ." he said with a yawn. "You want to make a good impression."

"Do I?" I swallowed hard, suddenly nervous from his observation.

He stretched his front legs until they slid out from under him. "Definitely seems like it."

"Ah, found them." I pulled out the khakis and quickly changed, shaking out some of my nerves in the process. "There. When I get home, we're going to the pet store."

He flopped to his side. "And then we'll do some investigating."

Chapter Twenty

Mrs. Roland was behind the counter stabbing flower stems into green foam. "Meredith! I so hoped I'd see you today. I could use all the help I can get."

"Where do you want me?"

She laughed. It sounded just like Jay's only quieter and at a higher octave. "Everywhere. How are you at arranging flowers?"

I shrugged. "I've done it on cakes before but never like how you're doing it."

She waved me over and then grabbed another flower from in front of her. "Good enough for me. If you can follow my style guide, then you'll do great." She held out a white carnation. I only knew the name because I used to buy these from the grocery store during college. Four flowers for a dollar was a great deal for a pop of color in my dorm room. Beyond that, my flower knowledge was limited to those I created for cakes (making me a bit of an oddity in a town known for its flora).

Mrs. Roland tapped the open book, displaying a diagram of where to place flowers along with a photo of what the finished product should look like. It was a large arrangement that would be set into a heavy-looking white vase—standard funeral style.

"I've got three more of these to do, and that's not counting what others have ordered to send their respects."

Following the diagram, I stuck the carnation into the green foam next to three pale-yellow daisies. "I never even thought about sending flowers."

"And that's absolutely fine. Nowadays, obituaries often mention donations to charities instead of flowers. It can get overwhelming for families. Many end up donating them to places that might like them. Nursing homes and the like."

"Did Gio's mention a charity?" I still hadn't looked at it.

"Nothing listed. Hence all the flowers."

"Shame. He used to donate our day-old breads to the regional food bank. Any extra pastries and cakes too." I smiled at the memory of dropping them off on occasion. Everyone volunteering for the organization would light up upon seeing the pastry boxes and bread bags. It wasn't much originally, and when it got to be too much, Gio had to reduce our baking load, but I bet it was appreciated all the same. Now the food bank and those it helped would go without. I'd have to tell whoever started the next bakery about that. Maybe they could continue.

Mrs. Roland set a block of foam on the counter and then reached down for several flowers in the buckets between us. "Too bad you didn't write it. Seems like you would have known where to send them. I know you hit a rough patch at the end, Rita and Jay both told me about what happened, but he still meant a lot to you, so I'm sorry for your loss."

"Thanks." No one had really said that to me yet. More they were sorry that I had been the one to find him. "Who did write his obituary?"

She stuck three flowers into the foam in quick succession. "His family lives somewhere in Fiddlefern Fjord, not too far away. So maybe one of them? Or possibly Naomi."

"Naomi would have known about the food bank." I reached down for more flowers, this time taking several like Mrs. Roland had done. I could go faster if I didn't have to grab a flower every time I placed one.

"It might not have been at the top of whoever's mind. Grief is like that." She would know. Her husband had died several years back when Rita and I were still in college.

"How do you stand it?" I asked after a few moments of quiet, the only noise coming from the foam being punctured. "All these flowers for such sad reasons."

"I like to think they're providing some relief. They let people know they're not alone in their grief. That can help immensely. I'd like to think flowers for any reason can be a bright spot." She picked up the arrangement, then carefully moved it to a table further back in the shop. I still had a few flowers left to go on mine, but when Mrs. Roland returned, she had two pieces of foam. She pushed one over to me. "Save you a trip."

"Thanks. Sorry I'm so slow."

"You think I was this fast right away?" She laughed. "I don't think so. You're doing just fine for your first arrangement. First day, week, even couple of weeks. You learn. You get faster. Even I need to rely on the book sometimes, and I've been at this since long before you were born."

She and Mr. Roland had taken over the shop from his parents once they were married. I'd heard the story plenty of times. He worked here with his parents, and she'd gotten a summer job here when they were teens. By the time school started back up, they were an item. She continued working at the flower shop, eventually doing so full-time after graduating. Mr. Roland went to school for business, then came back to the shop—and her. He proposed the day after he got his degree. It was a short engagement. The business ended up being a combined graduation and wedding present.

Finally I was done with my first arrangement, and after bringing mine across the shop to place it next to her finished one, I settled back in with another and found a rhythm. This one seemed to go faster, although Mrs. Roland was done long before I was and had moved on to other styles of arrangements.

"Back to your earlier comment," she began as I moved my flowers and then joined her at a stand where she was placing flowers in a wreath form, "it's true that we put together a lot of things for sad reasons, but we do plenty of floral arrangements and bouquets for happy times too. Weddings, showers, Valentine's Day, Mother's Day, and I do so love homecoming and prom season. It's a whole circle of life here. We provide comfort at the end, but we get to celebrate everything before then as well."

"We saw that in the bakery too. Cakes to celebrate, rolls for sandwiches for gatherings of all types, pastries and cookies for holidays and every day." Now who would fill that role for the town?

Our conversation moved on to other topics after that, happier ones. I hadn't spent this much time with Mrs. Roland in, well, ever. We'd talked over the years, of course (usually while I was waiting for Rita to finish getting ready), but never for this long. This, however, was hours of chitchatting, and it helped to pass the time. I was surprised when the buckets of flowers were once again empty and she didn't go back into the cooler for more.

She brushed her hands together, making a swoosh-clapping sound. "And we are all set."

"Already?" I surveyed the room, which was now full of bouquets and other floral arrangements.

A smile played on her lips. "You want to do more?"

"Do you need to do more? I don't want to leave if you have a bunch of other stuff to get done."

"Oh, I'm all good here. Really." She chuckled. "Tomorrow will be a big delivery day, but once I've brought everything to the funeral home, it will be almost like a normal day here. Although if you wouldn't mind, I have one delivery that needs to be made today. Floyd would usually do it since he lives closer, but you're in the area too."

"Sure. Where do you need me to go?"

"Naomi's." She turned and sorted through the counter of smaller bouquets and arrangements, then pulled out a pretty bundle of roses.

A knot formed in my stomach about seeing Gio's ex-wife. I'd intended to go check in on her, but now that I was being asked to, I was nervous. "Won't she be getting a lot of these flowers tomorrow?"

She wrapped the bouquet in protective cellophane and secured the stems. "Ah, yes, but these are different. She's going to want these."

I nodded. "Okay. I can do that. Where is Floyd anyway?"

"Left for the big flower expo in Boston. It's been years since I've gone. When I mentioned it to Floyd, he jumped at the chance. Brought the box truck with him, and I can't wait to see what he gets. Will probably be back sometime tomorrow."

I remembered how Rita would be gone for an entire week just before school started as her whole family went down for the show and to spend a few days playing tourist in the city. She and Jay would come home with a small potted plant for me and my parents. Mom loved to put them in the window above the kitchen sink.

Mrs. Roland looked around the room, hands on her hips, and sighed. "Course, him having the truck makes all these deliveries a bit more difficult."

"I can come back in the morning. My trunk's plenty big for these smaller arrangements, and I'm sure we can buckle the big ones in. Since I'm going to the funeral anyway, I might as well help you in the process."

She brightened. "Oh, that would be a big help, thank you. And thank you for everything you did today. I'd still be working if it weren't for you."

"Happy to do it, and if you ever need extra hands and I'm available, you know where to find me."

She handed me the wrapped bouquet. "I might just take you up on that." She motioned me to follow her as she walked back to the front counter where the cash register was, then pressed a button that released the drawer. She opened it, pulled out some money, and then pressed the bills into my hand.

"Are you sure? You're like family. We help when needed, no pay needed." Though it was appreciated.

"Of course I am. And you know me well enough to know I won't change my mind."

I held my arms out to protect the bouquet and gave Mrs. Roland a big hug. "It was great to see you today."

"Likewise. Hope to see more of you sometime."

"Well, you'll see me tomorrow." She stepped out of my hug, giving me a knowing look to say that wasn't what she meant. Not wanting to dive into that with her, I continued, "And thank you for this." I grabbed my bag from behind the counter and then made a show of sticking the money into my wallet.

"You earned it. Now go bring that bouquet to Naomi."

"I will." But first I was going to head home and grab Trubbs. Now that I had cash in hand and didn't need to wait for my paycheck to clear, we could head to the pet store after this delivery. He'd be happy to join me if I told him it was for the investigation.

Not that I'd be investigating. No, I was doing a favor for Mrs. Roland. But if, while making my delivery and giving Naomi my condolences, I asked her who she thought had killed Gio, that wouldn't be me investigating. It would be me just making conversation, right?

Yeah, let's call it that.

Chapter Twenty-One

Trubbs happily pranced next to me as I walked up the sidewalk on Naomi's street. She didn't live far from me at all, so I'd decided to walk and test Trubbs's ability to stay near me. We'd still go get him a leash and harness after this, but based on photos I'd seen on social media of other travel cats, I could imagine at least a few situations where we wouldn't have him leashed while out and about.

"So what do you need me to do?" Trubbs asked as we neared the house.

Remembering that Gio had once had a cat before he became anti cat fur, I asked, "Can you look for signs outside of her having a cat?" I wanted to keep him busy and hopefully out of trouble.

"I have to stay outside?"

"You usually don't bring your cat to other people's houses. It's not polite. What if they have allergies?"

We turned down the flagstone path of the small ranch home Gio had once shared with Naomi.

"Well, I can tell you she either has a cat or a little dog."

I looked down at the tabby. "How do you know?"

His tail curved forward, almost as if pointing. "There's a pet door right there on the front door. And I don't smell dog" —he made that weird smelling face that cats sometimes made, though it appeared to be more due to the mention of a dog than actually smelling anything—"so I assume cat." His tail went loose as it rose to its usual upright position. Maybe he actually had been pointing to the door.

"Still, cat or no cat, you can't come in with me. See what else you can find."

"Okay . . ." he grumbled before trotting off to the bushes in the front garden.

Satisfied that he'd be occupied out here, I took a deep breath to center myself, then strode up the rest of the path, bouquet in hand. I knocked on the door, and as I waited for it to open, I studied Naomi's car in the driveway. The same one she'd had since before the divorce. But there were no others. I felt bad. Had anyone beyond Rita checked up on her since yesterday? I remembered when my grandmother died. People dropped in on my grandfather for days so that he wasn't lonely. Mostly relatives, though. The neighbors came later on, after the funeral, once our family members who'd come in for it had gone back home.

Had the divorce really been so bad that no one in her circle cared that he died? Did she?

A new thought struck me as I heard footsteps stop at the front door. What if someone in her family had killed Gio, as payback for something that happened in the divorce?

"Meredith, is that you behind those flowers?" Naomi asked as the door opened.

Lost in thought, I hadn't realized the bouquet had drifted level to my nose, so I lowered it and smiled at Gio's ex-wife.

"Hi, Naomi. Mrs. Roland asked me to bring these to you. I'm so sorry about Gio."

She choked on a cry as she took the flowers and my arm, practically lifting me up the step into her house. "Oh, thank you so much for these. I never would have thought I'd get another one from him."

"Him?"

Still holding on to my hand, she pulled me into the kitchen, the front door falling shut behind us. "Gio. Throughout our marriage, he'd give me flowers on Saturdays. A way to always end the week on a high note no matter what had happened with the shop, my family, or even between us. Kept it up even after we started divorce proceedings and surprisingly for a couple years after it was final. Seeing you here today with that bouquet, the same kind he'd always send, I just knew." Her back was to me as she pulled out a footstool and then stood on it to dig a vase out of a cupboard above her fridge, but I could tell she'd wiped her eye with her hand. "She must have remembered after all this time and thought I'd appreciate the sentiment. Bless her."

Mrs. Roland hadn't made it seem like she was the one sending it, but the bouquet had been special by the way she told me to bring it here.

After looking at several vases and then putting them back in the cupboard, Naomi found one that must have suited her. "They always used to come with the vase, but after I realized it would be a regular thing, I told her to just send the flowers. I donated most of the vases but kept a few of the more unique ones. Now I'm glad I did."

She stepped down from the stool, then shuffled to the sink. We were quiet a moment as water filled the vase while Naomi prepped the bouquet. Now that the flowers weren't right in front of my nose, the smell of fresh-baked bread hung in the air, and the kitchen felt warmer than the rest of the house too. Although she'd cleaned the kitchen since finishing, she'd clearly been baking today. I hadn't realized she could. She was never back in the kitchens at Flour Power. Always worked in the shop while Gio concentrated his efforts on the food.

Once the vase was half full, Naomi moved it to the counter, placed the flowers inside, then washed her hands before turning off the water. She rubbed her eyes as she faced me once more.

"Thank you so much for bringing these."

"Of course, of course. How are you holding up? This can't be easy for you."

She sighed. "I'm hanging in there. As you can imagine, many don't think about the ex. They think I've moved on from him and don't need the condolences. And although I have moved on, Gio was a big part of my life for a long time, and I still cared about him." Grabbing the vase, she led me into the living room. She set the flowers on the mantel, then turned to me. "You have time to chat? Floyd isn't due back until late, and no one has been over today or even called besides my mother. At least if you don't count the police and that reporter friend of yours, which I don't." She sniffed. "I could really use the company, even if just for a little while. It's a Saturday, I'm sure you have plans."

"Only with my cat," I confessed, believing that would put her at ease. It made it sound like I had nothing going on. Trubbs, however, would still hold me to them no matter what. I glanced out the window and didn't see him anywhere. I hoped he was behaving during his investigation.

"Oh, you have a cat?"

I turned back to her. "Trouble. Got him a few weeks ago.

A silver tabby. You have one, right? I saw the pet door on my way in."

"Sure do. Spatch. Used to be Gio's and mine. Gio kept the bakery." A small look of satisfaction flashed momentarily across her face. "I kept him."

Nodding slowly, I took a spot on her couch as she sat across from me on a cushy recliner.

Her expression turned to one of sadness as she stroked the arm of the chair. "Kept this recliner too. Wouldn't fit in his apartment, and it was too comfy to get rid of."

"I think I remember Spatch." I hoped switching the topic would help cheer her up a bit. "He was that stray who hung around the bakery, right?"

When she brightened, I knew I had succeeded. "Such a scrawny thing he was. Course you couldn't tell that from all the cat fur. Made him look a lot bigger than he was. Now he's still wicked furry, but there's an eighteen-pound cat underneath it. I never imagined he'd get quite that big, but he eats all the time. Can't ever let the food bowl go empty on him, or he'll let me know about it. Loudly. Has no problem tapping me to tell me I'm taking too long to take care of it either. Those mittens of his are something to wake up to as well, let me tell ya."

Easily imagining the scene, I chuckled. "Trubbs likes to yap at me when his is empty too." Only he had no problem verbalizing that he could see any portion of the bottom of the bowl. And he wasn't some huge fluffy orange thing either.

"They're so funny, aren't they?" When I nodded, she continued, "He's a big ball of mush if you feed him, though. Took to Floyd after I started having him feed Spatch at night."

I crossed my legs and placed my hands on my thigh, wishing I had something to occupy them. A cup would do, but Naomi hadn't offered me anything to drink. It had probably slipped her mind with everything going on the last two days. I doubted entertaining unexpected guests ranked highly in her thoughts at the moment. It wouldn't for me.

"Now when you say Floyd, you mean florist Floyd? The guy who I filled in for today?"

A warm grin spread across her face. "That's him, all right. We've been together a little over a year now."

She seemed to drift off a moment as she stared out the window, then shook away whatever thought she'd been having and focused on me once more. "It's funny, really. It's because of Gio that I met him. He started delivering the bouquets. Every Saturday. He finally wore me down after a few months. Said I must have been wicked special if my ex-husband was still sending me flowers every week. We'd always chat for a few minutes, but soon his stays grew longer as those quick chats turned into full conversations. Eventually, he started bringing dinner with him in addition to the flowers. Nothing fancy, just something he could pick up before coming over."

By now, her grin had grown into a full-fledged smile. "Then one night he didn't leave. We've been together since then. Gio must have taken the hint because the flowers stopped coming a few weeks after."

It seemed a little weird to me that Mrs. Roland would send sympathy flowers to Naomi that were the same kind and style that her now-dead ex-husband would send her, but who was I to judge? "Mrs. Roland said he was at some flower show?"

"Yeah, terrible timing, huh?" Her smile fell. "He offered to come home right away once I called him, but he'd been so excited about going, and I knew Mrs. Roland was hoping he'd meet with some vendors and get new plants. I couldn't ask him to leave."

"But he'll be back tonight?"

"Yes. There's technically a grower's seminar tomorrow morning to close out the expo, but everything he promised he'd do got done, so he's going to skip that to make sure he's back in time for the funeral."

I gave her a sympathetic smile. "Are you going to be okay until he gets back? I could stay. We could order pizza or something." Trubbs would understand. For all I knew, he'd gotten bored and had wandered over to Robin's house for an early dinner with the stray cats that she fed.

She flapped her hand dismissively. "You don't need to worry about me. I have been baking all day to help calm my nerves and take my mind off things, so I have plenty to eat even if I have nothing to put on it."

"Maybe Floyd will bring something yummy back with him. Or you could call, and I bet he'd pick up butter or jelly on the way home." I smiled at her, relieved I wouldn't have to stay despite my offer.

She pursed her lips as she contemplated my suggestion, her eyebrows rising. "Now that is a good idea."

At that moment, a large orange cat pushed his way through the cat door. It was almost comical thinking something so big was coming through such a small door, but once he was inside, his fur semiflattened from his entrance, you could see he was smaller. Enough to not have trouble using the pet door at least.

He glanced over at Naomi, then shook, fluffing himself out once more.

"He's practically a lion!" Spatch had filled out since I'd last seen him, but there was no mistaking him and all that fur.

She laughed. "A grumpy one when his food bowl is empty. I should probably go check it." She stood, and I did the same.

"Thank you so much for bringing the flowers and staying to chat a bit. Under other circumstances . . ."

"I understand. It was good seeing you, Naomi."

"See you tomorrow? It would be nice knowing that I'm going to see a friendly face."

I nodded. "Wouldn't miss it." Especially if Gio's killer could be there.

Smiling, she saw me to the door. As soon as I stepped outside, Spatch meowed loudly for more food, and Naomi hurriedly closed it behind me, telling the cat to be patient.

I knew how having a demanding cat was. Speaking of, where was he?

Chapter Twenty-Two

Trubbs sat glowering at the end of the driveway, staring at the cat door. "I don't like that fat cat. He always gobbles up every last bite," he whined. "Doesn't care if other cats are around who need it more. At least *I* wait. I know I have you. And he has a person too."

"He had a rough start in life," I began as I started down the sidewalk. "Didn't always know where his next meal was coming from. Or when. That causes food issues for some even after the cause is no longer a problem."

I thought back to how Trouble rushed over to the communal cat food the day I got him. "I seem to remember you going so fast to get to the crunchies at the cat café that you crashed into the bowls and tipped them over."

Trubbs stopped, forcing me to as well, and looked up at me. "Spilling it means more of us could get it at one time."

I didn't know what to say to that, and a single, "Oh," escaped. Where had he learned that? He hadn't been forthcoming about where he was before the Feline Familiar Cat Café.

Seemingly knowing I was struggling with my thoughts, he replied, "Yeah," then resumed walking, his tail flicking over his back as if waving me forward. "Can we go home first? I'm hungry."

"Okay." At least going back to the apartment meant we could get my car first and I wouldn't end up carrying twenty pounds of cat food home over my shoulder. Hadn't thought about that before leaving for Naomi's.

I wondered if I should start leaving an outside food bowl for Trubbs in case he ever couldn't get back inside for some reason or if he knew of another cat in need of food. Hopefully my parents wouldn't mind.

After an early dinner and a lobster treat for Trubbs and a sandwich for me (although I now really wanted pizza after mentioning it to Naomi) we drove down to the pet store.

"Please, please, please don't get into trouble here," I said as I pulled into a parking spot along Main Street near the store. "I don't want to have to drive out to the bigger pet store if I don't have to."

"If this is what it's going to take to get to travel with you when you go places, I'll be on my best behavior. I promise."

And he was. Even though he'd promised, I'd expected a little mischief. But no, he sat in the top part of the shopping cart where kids usually sat, facing away from me with his paws up on the backrest, and let me push him around without incident.

Not without commentary, however.

"Now this is the life," he said as we perused the aisles, going up and down each one. "I don't even have to move and I'm going places."

What did he think he'd be doing when we went in the car?

Soon, the cart was filling up. Food, both dry and canned. Toys. Even more toys. New cat litter. A scratching post and small cat tree that would allow him to better see out my back window. I was splurging now that Mrs. Roland had given me some money for helping her, but it was also easy to do with Trubbs' ability to tell me what he wanted.

I pointed out the harnesses for his inspection.

He eyed the rack. "Blue. No, I want green."

"Green? Okay." I grabbed the green one, immediately spotting one difference between this one and the others in the display. "You know this one comes with a collar, right? If we get it, you have to wear it." It was also more expensive, but I doubted he cared about that element.

"But look at it. It's got a fancy bow tie. You don't have to put it on me all the time. Maybe just when we go out." He turned to face me and stood, putting his front paws on the handle of the cart and getting as close to me as possible. "Please?"

"We should try it on first." I didn't want to spend the money on it if he wasn't going to wear it despite his bargaining with me.

His reply was immediate. "Okay."

Maybe he was serious about this. I glanced over my shoulder, checking to see that we were alone in the aisle as I slipped the collar out from the package. Trubbs straightened as I brought it to his neck and secured it around him. I sucked in my lips to stop my immediate reaction.

Aww...

Trouble was made for bow ties.

He tapped me, then sat back in the seat. "Well?"

"You want to see?"

"Of course I do." He leaned in as I pulled out my phone, then sat up straight when he saw me turn the screen toward him. I just as easily could have taken a picture and shown him, but this was Trubbs. He wasn't an ordinary cat. Pivoting this way and that as he tried to keep his eyes on my phone, he said, "Oh, yes. I do so like the green."

Nodding in agreement, I said, "You're very handsome. You were right about the green. And you'll wear it when we go places?"

"I would even wear it in the neighborhood." He lifted his head but kept his gaze on the phone screen. "I know another cat or two who wished they'd look this good in a collar like this."

That was as good of an endorsement as any. "All right, we'll get it."

"Oh, isn't he handsome," a familiar voice said from behind me, causing me to jump. "Sorry about that, Meredith."

I spun around to face Charlotte Kirk, the owner of the pet store. "Didn't even hear you."

"It's the shoes. I try not to wear things that squeak across the floors. Sets the dogs off. Who do you have with you?"

When I glanced back at Trubbs, I would have sworn he was smiling, either at my surprised reaction and rapidly beating heart or at having someone else call him handsome.

Turning to look at Charlotte once more, I gave her a sheepish smile. "Sorry for taking the collar out of the package. I wanted to see how he looks, and I do plan on buying it. Just let me slip it off him and I'll bring it to the register."

Charlotte put up a hand to stop me. "Of course you're getting it. He looks too good for you to not, so I wouldn't even worry about trying to get it back into the packaging. You might as well try the harness on while you're here just to be sure that fits, see how it adds to the whole look. Bet he'll be even cuter."

"Oh, I like her," Trubbs said from his spot on the cart. He reached out for her with his paw, letting it hang in midair as she was a few feet away and out of reach. I was reminded of

Naomi talking about Spatch's big mittens. Trouble was a good size, but still smaller than the furry orange tabby. It was hard to judge how much so with all that fur.

"Oh, isn't he darling." Charlotte stepped closer to us so she could scratch his head.

"Oh, he's something, that's for sure. All right, you heard her, Trubbs. Let's try on the harness and make sure it fits you."

It took some figuring out, but I finally got the harness on him. I had no idea what I was doing and had twice sent his front legs through the wrong hole. And either he wasn't helping because Charlotte was there and he wanted to act more like a cat for his audience (who kept heaping praise on him) or he was just being a cat. Sometimes I couldn't tell, but I chalked it up to us both not knowing what we were doing with the harness. Next time it would go more smoothly. And there would be a next time as once we succeeded in getting it on, Charlotte confirmed it was a good fit.

She continued to fawn over his good manners once we got to the counter to check out, and she gave him a treat because he'd been so good.

"Yours are better," he quipped over the tiny treat from the bag. "I'd need about five of these per one of yours."

That was not in my budget. Lobster was probably cheaper than buying the number of bags it would take to equal one batch's worth according to his math. One bag, however, would at least hold me over through tomorrow and Gio's funeral. I reached for the sealed bags sitting on a stand on the counter, then pushed it toward the rest of my stuff.

It was then I noticed a collection jar sitting next to the stand. On it was a photo of the missing cow. "What are you raising money for with the cow? I thought we were just supposed to call the police if we saw him."

"I've heard about him," Trubbs quipped from the cart.

I shot him a questioning glance at the same time as Charlotte *awwed*, then said, "Isn't that cute! He wants to be a part of the conversation." She and I looked back at one another, and she explained, "The steer has been on the loose for a month and a half already. He deserves to live out his life if he ever is caught and not go to the meat market. An animal sanctuary has agreed to let him live on their ranch if we can raise the initial funds for his care."

"Oh, that's great to hear. He's become a bit of a local celebrity, hasn't he? Dodging those going looking for him, only being spotted under the disguise of night."

Finished with ringing me out, she laughed and handed me my change and receipt. "Next he'll start going around in oversized sunglasses and a wide-brim hat to hide his face."

"Like some cartoon spy. Well, I hope he is found soon. At least we've been having good weather." I dropped my coins into the cylindrical container. "And I love the idea of him going to a sanctuary. Maybe I could take Trubbs for a visit. Sounds like something my blog's readers would love."

"They certainly would. Thank you for your donation. And yes, still call the police if you see him. They're on board with the plan."

Charlotte handed me the bag of smaller items, and I placed it in the top part of the cart next to Trubbs, then heaved the large bag of food into the lower portion. Waving over my shoulder as I walked away, I told her to have a nice day. She said nothing to me, instead telling Trubbs to come back anytime.

We headed back to my car, and just as I was closing the trunk, the box truck with the logo for Mrs. Roland's florist company passed by in a hurry.

"He's earlier than I thought he would be."

"Who is?" Trubbs asked, still sitting in the cart in his bow tie and harness.

"Floyd. Naomi said he'd be back late." I shrugged. "He probably wanted to get here as soon as he could to be with her. I should go tell him about stopping to pick up some jelly to bring home just in case she couldn't reach him. Reception can be spotty on the road."

I pushed the cart back to the front of the store and waved goodbye to Charlotte through the window.

"Come on," I said to Trubbs as I snapped the new leash we got to his harness. Then I placed him on the sidewalk beside me. "Ready for a test run?"

Chapter Twenty-Three

Floyd was just closing the back door of the van as I approached.

"Hi, Floyd," I called from several feet away, startling him. Glad to know I wasn't the only one who was so jumpy. He wasn't from here originally but had called the place home since I was in high school. He was Jay's age, part of the reason why I'd been surprised by Naomi's admission that they were a couple now. She was at least ten years older than me.

"Oh, hi, Meredith. How are you?" He slung a duffel bag over his shoulder.

"Good. I didn't think you'd be back so soon. Naomi said you'd be in late."

He grinned sheepishly. "I may have driven a little faster than I should have. Please don't tell Mrs. R. I kind of wanted to get home, you know?"

I nodded in understanding. "My lips are sealed. Does Naomi know that you're already here?"

His sheepish look remained as he shook his head. "I told

her I was a little further out than I was to give her a nice surprise."

"Did she mention needing jelly or butter to you?" He looked at me quizzically. Chuckling, I replied, "I'll take that as a no. Well, you might want to grab some to add to the surprise of you being back earlier. She has been baking a lot today but had nothing to put on the bread. I offered to stay and order pizza with her, but she turned me down."

"Thanks for the heads-up"—he reached out and placed his hand on my upper arm—"and thanks for checking up on her. I'm sure it's been a rough day."

"Yeah, I had planned on going earlier, but then I ended up helping Mrs. Roland with all the flower arrangements for tomorrow."

Floyd made a show of wiping his forehead with the back of his hand. "Phew. Glad she had the help. We've been short-handed lately, not sure if she mentioned that, and me being gone at the show didn't help."

"She wouldn't have let you work today even if you had been here." I gave him a kind smile. "You would have been with Naomi. Anyway, Mrs. Roland asked if I could deliver some flowers to her, so it all worked out."

"Oh, someone sent her flowers?" He brightened and seemed almost relieved. "That's nice that somebody would think of her. She was worried nobody would think of the ex-wife in all of this mess."

Mess. That was one way to describe this whole situation. "I guess they were from Mrs. Roland actually, something about them being the same type of flowers that Gio used to send her." I shrugged. "She must have thought it would be a nice way to remember him."

Something flashed across Floyd's face, not anger, I didn't think, more annoyance, but he quickly covered it with a strained smile. "That was nice of her." He paused, his smile turning genuine. "That's actually how I first met Naomi, the flowers."

"Yeah, she was telling me. It's a really cute story. And that's how we got on the subject of pizza. A real dinner would probably do her some good."

He slowly lifted his chin, a love-sick grin growing across his face. "Ah. Now I understand. Pizza sounds good. I'm starving. She always changes up her order, but I think I know exactly what to get her this time."

Usually, I'd have suggested calling to see what she'd want (I'd want a choice if it were me), but I believed the surprise would be good for her. "She's really going to be glad to see you."

He sputtered a laugh. "Might all depend if I'm right about the pizza. Let me call in that order right now." As he dug into his pocket, he seemed to notice Trubbs for the first time, who was intently smelling his shoes. "You got a new cat."

I laughed. "What was your first clue? This is Trouble." At the mention of his name, Trubbs reached up for me, sitting on his hind legs as he lifted both front paws. I squatted to pick him up, then stood once more.

He'd been so quiet I had barely noticed he was there, but as I adjusted him in my arms, he whispered, "His shoes stink."

What shoes didn't stink to a cat?

Floyd chuckled as he reached out to let Trubbs sniff his hand. "Aren't they all trouble? Spatch is always getting into something, and with that long fur, it gets everywhere. I'm gone for two days and look"—he pointed to the sleeve of his outstretched arm—"I still have it on me."

"I know how that is, and he's only got short fur."

Trubbs, done with his sniff investigation, turned away from Floyd and then crawled up over my shoulder. "His shirt smells like that cat." He headbutted me. "You still do too, but I'll allow it given the circumstances." And I hadn't even petted Spatch while I was there. All I'd done was sit on the couch.

Floyd lowered his arm now that Trubbs had lost interest. "All right, well, I should get to ordering that pizza."

"Before I go, I told Mrs. Roland that I would help her load all the flowers tomorrow morning and get them to the funeral. She wasn't expecting you back tonight."

"I called her earlier to let her know I was heading home. I can take care of it. No worries."

I shook my head. "Please don't think I'm going to back out of my offer to help. I have no problem hauling some flowers around. You stay with Naomi."

He pressed his palms together, sandwiching his phone between them. "Thank you. Although they hadn't been together in a long time, I know tomorrow is going to be hard for her."

I gave Floyd a sympathetic smile. Then to break up the somber shift of the conversation, I added, "But with the van, things will be much easier now."

Nodding, he said, "That's for sure."

"Hey, you didn't see anything strange that morning, did you? You were probably grabbing the van around the same time it happened."

Floyd shook his head. "Wish I could say I did, but it was just the expected sort of stuff. A few dog walkers, a guy on a skateboard, some early-morning joggers. Can't believe I used to get up that early to run in high school for cross country."

"Running was never my thing. Gym class was bad enough. I could never do it for fun."

"I certainly wouldn't now." He chuckled, tapping his barely there stomach. "Too many carbs thanks to Naomi. But hey, maybe you could come work with us if you liked it today. I heard about you getting fired, though given what happened, guess you'd probably need a job now no matter what. Sorry for your loss, whichever one you're more upset about."

"Oh, thanks." I wasn't sure how to take that apology. Not for the first time, I wondered what was going to happen to the bakery with Gio gone. Only this time, I'd said it out loud to someone else.

"Naomi's talking to her lawyer about it. See if there was anything in the divorce papers about it." He replied with a shrug. "Doubt there will be anything based on what she's told me before."

I didn't think he thought he'd revealed anything major, just the idea that an ex-wife was interested in her now-dead ex-husband's business dealings to see if any of it would affect her. But what if there was more to it than that? Had he implied that Naomi wanted the bakery? Was that what all of her baking today had been about? Not a way to keep busy as she dealt with her grief but the practicing of recipes new and old so that she could take over Flour Power? She'd never set foot in its kitchen before. So why the sudden urge to do so now? And would she have killed Gio over it?

The sinking feeling in my gut told me it was time to leave. "All right, well, I have a full trunk of pet supplies and you have a pizza to order. I'm sure I'll see you tomorrow, but I'm glad I caught you tonight. Naomi is going to be thrilled." It almost hurt me to say that last part. Had I just made sure Gio's killer got her dinner? Unable to stay a moment longer, I gave him a quick wave and said good night before turning back the way I'd come.

"Come on, Trubbs. Let's get home."

Chapter Twenty-Four

"I am so sorry I'm late," I gasped out of breath as I ran into the flower shop. "Mom came down to ask about riding together to the funeral later, and you know how she can get." She'd tried to insist there was no reason to bring two cars, even saying that I might not be up to driving home afterward. Finally, I told her I'd probably stay longer than she and Dad would want to, so I could catch up with the other bakers and the girls from the shop. I couldn't tell her I was going to do some investigating while I was there. And I certainly couldn't say that Trubbs was going to the funeral too. Not that he'd be coming inside. He was in charge of his own investigation.

Mrs. Roland flapped a hand at me. "You're right on time." She picked up an arrangement from the counter, and once I grabbed one of my own, I followed her out to the van. "Thank you for coming to help. I'm sure Floyd appreciates it."

"He's where he needs to be." With a possible murderer. I wondered if I should tell Jay about Naomi wanting the bakery or if he already knew.

Mrs. Roland lifted the latch of the van's back door, then groaned.

"What's wrong?" I asked.

"Locked. Keys are in my pocket. Can you grab them? My hands are full." She turned and looked at me. With a chuckle, she said, "Oops, yours are too." She walked over to the back stairs of the shop and then set the arrangement on the top step. She hurried back to unlock the van, and once the doors were wide open, she took the arrangement from my hands.

As she secured it inside the van, I ran back to the one she had put down.

"Sorry about that," she said once I'd returned. "I forget he locks everything. Guess he never lost the habit after moving here."

My mind flashed to how the door of Flour Power had been locked when it usually wasn't at that hour. Gio had moved here after meeting Naomi and thought we were all foolish for not locking our doors even though he'd come from a small town guilty of doing the same. He diligently locked the bakery every night, but as soon as he was in the building, everything was unlocked. So was Gio's killer not from here, at least not originally? Adam was from here, though I doubted a locked door would be enough to remove him from a list of suspects.

"I should be better at locking up, but I'm not." Mrs. Roland added quietly, then looked around as if someone might be nearby to overhear. "Don't tell Davis."

I cracked a smile. "Davis might be an insurance agent, but I doubt even he locks his front door."

She laughed as she took the arrangement from me. While she secured it in the van, I went back into the store to grab more flowers. Unsure what to take next and sure Mrs. Roland had a plan for it all, I waited a moment, taking in the small shop. The morning sun streamed through the windows, illuminating the petals of the flowers she had displayed on stands and shelves and hanging in the windows. It reminded me of stained glass at a cathedral I'd visited once during a sunrise tour just to see the morning light strike it just right. I breathed in deeply. The smell was nowhere near as overwhelming as it had been yesterday. Turning around as the back door opened, I thought about Floyd's suggestion. I could see myself working here if Mrs. Roland asked me to.

"It's beautiful here in the mornings," I told her once she walked into the room.

She smiled reverently as she looked around. "My favorite time of day. Mr. Roland proposed to me one morning like this." After another moment in which I doubted she saw me standing there, she sighed wistfully. "All right, let's get the rest of this loaded."

The ride to the funeral home was silent. Mrs. Roland still seemed to be lost in thought with her memories, and I was wading through my own. It hadn't been long since seeing my last dead body, but that had been a stranger. This was Gio. And my first funeral since my grandmother's when I was a kid. I didn't like funerals, but who did? Well, aside from those who worked them, although *like* probably wasn't the right word.

I bet Gio's killer would like this one too. If they were from town, they'd be there. Maybe I'd have to focus on those who seemed to be too happy today.

The delivery went easily enough. The staff at Underhill Funeral Home had a good system for unloading things, complete with a trolley cart, so we only needed two trips from the van to bring all the flowers inside. I followed Mrs. Roland's lead once inside, carrying whatever she needed me to and putting it where she or one of the Underhills directed.

This side of a funeral I'd never seen before. The getting ready portion before chairs were even set up. Before the framed photos. Before the snacks for those milling about or waiting in line. Would there be snacks? We used to make them at Flour Power. Nothing elaborate. A lot of one-bite treats. Who would make them now?

And Gio was there. Well, his body was. I didn't see it. Didn't want to. But before we left, I promised Gio his killer would be found.

"I don't know why this is so hard for me," I told Trubbs as I slipped into my black pants. "I mean, he fired me the last time I saw him. We didn't get along."

"If that's what you need to tell yourself to help you get through the day, that's fine." Trubbs slowly blinked at me, and he maintained the look as he continued, "But before that, he was someone you looked up to. I remember you packing your list of new foods to try with samples to give him from your last trip."

Trubbs was right, but "He shot me down and wouldn't even let me try to make them for him to taste. Never mind put them on the menu. He stifled me." Ugh, why couldn't I let this go?

"Did he?" He opened his eyes and flicked his tail.

"What does that mean?" If he'd been trying to get me to not be sad about Gio's death, then he was doing a great job at it. I clenched my jaw and breathed out hard.

"You kept trying. You didn't give up. Sounds like he was challenging you."

"Oh, he was challenging, all right." I sighed. "I just wanted to show him how we could make Flour Power better."

Trubbs jumped onto my dresser, missing everything I had up there and proving he could be graceful when he wanted. "You were trying to do things your way and going behind his back to do it."

I pulled my blouse over my head. "I wasn't expecting to get a lecture from my cat."

"And I wasn't expecting to give one."

Still annoyed, I turned toward the mirror to fix my hair and popped the clip that had been holding it up off.

Trubbs stepped toward me and headbutted my side. "I was hoping to make you feel better about him. So much for that. I'm sorry. I know your feelings are still sore about being fired. Never mind finding him like that. But maybe your firing was as much about you as him."

With the clip in my mouth, I said, "Him?"

"It was something your mom said."

I pulled the clip from my mouth. "When?"

"The day with the lobster monster."

Although I was trying to keep still as I placed the clip back in my hair, I couldn't help but chuckle at the name. "But you weren't there."

"You didn't see me, that's all." He glanced at himself in the mirror. "Can you put my collar on me today?"

I nodded. "Where were you?"

He licked his paw, then used it to clean behind his ear. "I'd come back because of the smell and heard you talking with your mom about making the lobster bruschetta. Whatever that is."

"Bread with oil and tomatoes—"

"Not important." His nose twitched. "But she talked about risk."

"I remember. She didn't want to risk not liking the bruschetta, so she didn't bother trying. That's silly." While looking in the mirror, I turned right and then left to make sure I was presentable. No cat fur anywhere. Gio wouldn't have approved otherwise.

"Silly to you. But it was a risk for her. Just like you changing the recipe on Gio was a risk that you took for him. That wasn't your call to make. That would be like me trying to push another cat up the tree when he wanted to run across the road like he always did to get away from the dog chasing us."

"Are you speaking from experience?" I scratched around his face and under his chin. "Because I'd prefer it if you didn't run out into the road or bother the neighborhood dogs."

"I look both ways, remember? And besides that, I was the one wanting to go up the tree. But focus. What I'm saying is you weren't Gio's boss. He was yours. He would have taken the fall if your changes didn't work out, not you. I didn't know that cat was afraid of heights because it had gotten stuck up in a tree for two days. You don't know what may have caused Gio to be risk averse. You can't choose someone's risks for them. So once you challenged him openly, he had to take a stand and prove to you that your changes weren't risks he was willing to take. But someday, if you go back to baking after all of this, you can take your own risks."

I raised my index finger, giving Trouble a one-minute gesture, and hurried out of the room. In my rush to the kitchen, his words finally began to sink in, my feet slowing with the weight of the realization. Anything I did was going to reflect on Gio. He'd been letting me get away with the lemon curd—maybe it was better—but I should have gone about it a different way. My insistence that he change things and take risks had led to my firing. That was on me.

"And if you don't go back to baking," Trubbs called after

me loud enough so I could still hear, "well, there will be other risks with whatever it is you choose to do in life."

I grabbed his collar from the drawer in the side table by the door and returned to my bedroom, where he was still waiting for me on the dresser.

"Okay, you're right," I admitted. He sat up straight as I put on his collar. "How are you so smart? They didn't estimate you to be that old."

He flicked his tail as he turned to face the mirror. "You know cats don't age like people do. I'm practically your age."

"Huh. I thought you were a teenager or something with the way you get into trouble."

"Ha! Even dogs age differently than you think." He tilted his head this way and that as he looked at his reflection. "And before you ask, yes, I did learn that at the café."

"Huh," I repeated, then waited as he continued to gaze in the mirror. "Are you done admiring yourself? We have work to do."

We still didn't know why Gio had been killed, and we certainly didn't know who murdered him. But I owed it to Gio to take a risk and find out.

Chapter Twenty-Five

"You remember what you need to do?" I asked Trubbs as we pulled into a parking spot at the funeral home and put the car in park.

He was already scoping out the other early arrivals from his seat. He craned his neck to look out the side window. I released his pet seat belt, and he rushed to the window to stand with his front paws against it. "Did you really have to put me in that for such a short trip? I can't see as well sitting down."

"It's good to get used to it while doing short drives. Then we can adjust it as needed before going on a longer trip." I'd have to research some other sort of safety gear if the belt didn't get better for him. "You didn't answer my question."

"Yes, I know what to do. Smell for those with cats and see who has a lot of fur on their legs. This would be a lot easier if I knew what type of cat we were looking for."

He wasn't wrong.

"All I know is the fur didn't match yours. So all long fur or short fur that isn't silvery white and black." I reached across the seat and unsnapped his harness.

Trubbs stepped out of it, then scratched at his shoulder with a hind paw. When he was done, he turned back to me. "How do I look?"

Chuckling, I straightened his collar. "Like you work here. Mr. Underhill wears bow ties too. Ready?"

"Let's do this."

I opened my door. Trubbs bounded out from around me as I exited the car. He trotted along the perimeter of the parking lot, where he'd eventually hit the lawn and the walkway to the front door. Hopefully no one had seen his exit. We weren't together. His cover story (that he'd insisted on having) was that he was a comfort cat. He'd greet people on the path outside the entryway. "No one can pass up a cat in a bow tie," he'd told me. I know I couldn't. He didn't know it yet, but I'd already ordered him bow ties in blue, red, and yellow. So much for my strict budget, but it had been a tough few days.

I hung back a moment to put on a better pair of shoes. The ones I only wore for things like this and didn't feel comfortable driving in. By the time I was done, a few more people had pulled into the lot and were getting out of their cars. But that was a good thing. I hadn't wanted to be the first person in so I could see Trouble in action.

"Meredith!" a familiar voice called after a few moments.

I turned to find Stacey and Roni crossing the parking lot. Waving at them, I stopped to let them catch up to me.

Stacey wrapped me up in a hug. "How are you doing?"

"Okay, all things considered." I put one arm around her and held out the other for Roni, then brought her into the hug. "How are you two?"

They stepped out of our group embrace. "Same," Stacey

said. "Still so surreal. We should be finishing up our baking for the day right now and cleaning the kitchen."

Roni nodded in agreement. "How's the job hunt?"

I told them about helping Mrs. Roland.

"I have a job at Botanical Bistro," she replied. "Line cook."

"I'm still looking," Stacey began, "but I have an interview at Leafs soon."

That should have been the first place I'd applied to. My prior experience as a barista during college would have given me a leg up on the competition. But I knew that too much of my paycheck would have gone back into the amazing coffee at Leafs and Grounds, a regional company that had opened a new location here a few months ago.

Stacey linked her arms through mine and Roni's. "Come on, ladies, let's go pay our respects."

"Oh my goodness, how cute is that cat!" Roni said with a squeal as we approached the front door.

Trouble sat up straighter and glanced our way at her reaction. "Why, thank you," he said through a chirpy meow, not that Roni or Stacey had heard it.

"He's wearing a bow tie!" Stacey gushed. She bent forward, pulling Roni and me with her as she tried to reach out for Trubbs. "I could never get Milo to wear one of these."

Trubbs took a step forward to accept the head scratches from her and turned it this way and that as she moved to under his chin. "She's got a cat, but she's clean about it. No fur. I'd say she's clear," he told me. "You should bring them by sometime, though. She gives good pets."

I bit my lip at his second comment as both of the girls *awwed* at his loud purrs. I hadn't thought they'd done anything to Gio—hadn't thought anyone in Wisteria Falls was capable of murder, really—but it was good to get confirmation.

"We should probably head in," I said, trying to stand. "We're causing a line." And Trubbs needed to do his job.

Stacey glanced over her shoulder. "Oh, you're right. Whoops." She gave Trubbs one more pet, as did Roni, before standing.

Mr. Underhill opened the door for us, shaking his head as we walked through, but a small smile crossed his face. "Everyone has been doing that."

Stacey gave him an amused look. "What do you expect when you dress up your cat and stick him at the door?"

"That's the thing. He's not ours," Mr. Underhill replied. "Showed up a little while ago. Everyone loves him, though. Might have to think about giving this cat a job."

"He already has one," I said, not thinking.

Mr. Underhill chuckled. "Yes, it seems he does." In a more somber tone, he added, "Thank you for coming," then directed us down the hall to the room I'd set up flowers in earlier.

A couple dozen people were in the room now, which looked much more how I'd expected it would. Frames with photo collages in them sat on easels, lining one wall. An overhead projector was casting videos on the back wall. People dotted the chairs here and there, but most were standing talking to one another or waiting in line to express their condolences to Gio's family. Five people stood at another line in the front, starting with who I assumed were his parents, then siblings. Two men stood behind two of the women, husbands no doubt. A third sister stood without a partner next to her siblings at the end of the line.

Stacey, Roni, and I went into the line first. As we inched forward, I perused the photos. Gio as a kid, many of the photos showing him baking. Christmas cookies with an older woman and his sisters. Cutting into a birthday cake as a teenager, one of his sisters wearing a tiara. Photos of school events and milestones. Graduation from high school. Him holding awards next to chocolate displays and gorgeous cakes. Several wedding photos. I smiled at the picture of him and Naomi getting the keys to Flour Power. Seemed she hadn't been forgotten.

Stacey gently elbowed me, then pointed to a photo. "Hey, there you are."

It was a photo of Gio and me in the kitchen. "The tenth anniversary of him having Flour Power."

"Two years ago?"

I shook my head. "Three. That was my second year there."

Finally it was our turn to greet his family. These sorts of things always made me feel so awkward, but it wasn't about me.

The first daughter leaned over to her mother as the people in front of us moved further down the line, and the mom's eyes lit up.

"Now, these are some faces I recognize." Gio's mother's voice was laced with sadness, but the smile on her face was genuine. "Thank you so much for coming."

"Wouldn't not come," I said. "So sorry for your loss."

Stacey, Roni, and I introduced ourselves to Gio's family, shaking hands or hugging each member of his family.

I stopped at the youngest sibling. "Gina, right?"

She nodded, then wrapped me in a hug. "It's been years since I've seen you."

I couldn't stop staring at her hair. The purple complemented her olive skin tone beautifully and was a bright spot in the sea of blacks and other darker, more subdued shades of clothing.

She let me go and took half a step back as she slid a hand

along the buzzed side of her head. Her hair fell to ear length on the other side. "Really different from when I helped Gio that summer."

A couple years younger than I was, she'd spent a summer with Gio and Naomi back when I was still working in the shop during culinary school. She'd worked with me out front and in the kitchen doing anything Gio would let her.

I smiled at her, remembering her long dark-brown, almost black hair in various styles of braids that summer. "I like it. What are you up to now?"

"I work in a bakery in Heartwood Hollow."

"Joanie's place?"

Her eyes widened. "Yeah, Suncraft Bakery. You know Joanie?"

"She's one of my closest friends from culinary school. You'll have to tell her hello for me."

She smiled. "I will. She'll be happy I ran into you."

I glanced over my shoulder—Stacey and Roni were no longer next to me—then pulled Gina in for another hug. "Looks like I'm holding up the line. I really am sorry about your brother."

"Thanks. He always liked you, you know. Said you were a talented baker with a lot of ideas. He looked forward to seeing what you'd do once you made those ideas your own." She patted my back and then stepped out of our hug, turning to greet the next person waiting to express their condolences.

I walked away speechless, passing Gio's casket where two people were currently kneeling, and went to find my mom.

Chapter Twenty-Six

I found Mom talking to Mrs. Roland and Mrs. Hopkins, the town manager of Wisteria Falls, but everyone called her the mayor. Mrs. Hopkins wrapped me in a hug. The mom of my childhood babysitter, she'd known me forever and had been there when my grandmother died years ago and there again recently on a trip when a man on our tour bus passed away in the seat behind me.

"We have to stop meeting like this," she said. "How are you doing?"

"I'm doing okay, actually." Finding Gio's killer would make me even better. "Thank you. How are you?"

She sighed worriedly. "This doesn't make the town look good, the murder of our local baker. But we'll make it through."

She let me go, and I took a step back. "Do you know what's going to happen with Flour Power?" Maybe she had some inside information.

She shook her head. "It was fully paid for. I did ask about that since the town was involved in helping him secure it from Max. So it's up to if Gio had a will or not. Certainly is a prime spot on Main Street for whatever goes in there next. I'm pulling for a bakery, though. Where else will we get our snacks for the town meetings?"

"You'll think of something in the meantime, I'm sure. Good to see you, Mrs. Hopkins." I turned to my mom. "Can I talk to you for a minute?"

She gave me a small nod before glancing at the other two ladies. "Excuse me a moment." She put her hand on my upper back, and we walked several feet away to an unoccupied portion of the wall. She looked me right in the eye, concern lacing her gaze as she studied me. "Do we need your father?"

"No, just you."

"Are you okay?"

I shrugged. Probably my most honest answer to that question. "We weren't just talking about you when we were talking about the lobster bruschetta, were we?"

"The bruschetta?" Then she seemed to remember, and she shook her head. "You got me. I can't begin to imagine what you are going through after these last few days, but I hate to think that your last encounter with Gio wasn't a good one. He may have fired you, and as much as I hate to say it because you're my daughter, I think he had reason to with the way you were going on."

I nodded. "I shouldn't have changed the recipes. I could take that risk if it were my bakery, but it wasn't."

"You wanted it to be."

I shrugged again. Was that what I wanted? "I just wished that he could have seen Flour Power for what it could be like I did."

She hugged me, and I threw my arms around her, tears welling for the first time. "He always liked you," she soothed.

"I hope your last encounter with him doesn't change how you feel about him."

"Of course not, Mom. He frustrated me a lot at the end, but I get it now. Gio gave me my start, and no matter where I end up from here, I'll be wicked grateful for that." I squeezed her tight before dropping my arms and pulling out from her hug. Wiping my eyes, I said, "Everyone's perfume is getting to me."

She gave me an understanding smile but said nothing about my bluff. I hated crying. I hated being seen crying even more. "All good?"

With my eyes finally (mostly) dry, I nodded firmly. "Yeah. Thanks, Mom."

At that moment, I caught sight of Adam coming through the open entryway of the room. He was with his mom and younger brother, Ryan, who was home from college for the summer. Their dad and older brother were likely out on the lobster boat. Ryan had a bright-green cast on his wrist with a couple signatures scrawled on it.

Giving Mom one last quick hug, I said, "I gotta go talk to someone, and you should get back to your friends." Left unsaid was why I had to talk to Adam.

Adam's eyes lit up when he saw me. "Hey, how was that lobster?"

"My cat loved it, thank you."

Ryan turned to me. "Your cat?"

"Yeah. I'm allergic to lobster. He's not. Made him some treats."

"Did you see the cat outside?"

A grin played on my lips. "I did."

He snorted a laugh. I couldn't tell if it was from amusement or mockery.

I glanced at Adam. "Were you able to get your last

paycheck yet? Mine just came out of evidence." I didn't want to give it away that I knew his hadn't been in the pile that morning.

"Ouch." He made a face. "How long did that take?"

"Longer than I wanted it to, but I took a picture of it, and it's in my account now, so that's good."

"Good. Yeah, Gio mailed mine." He pursed his lips to the side and shrugged. "Can't blame the guy for not wanting to see me again. Guess it worked out, though. Might have put me at the scene of the crime otherwise, huh?"

"Yeah, imagine that." Seemed he hadn't heard that I'd found Gio. I wasn't going to tell him. But if Adam already had his check, there was no point in him going to the bakery unless he went with the explicit purpose to kill Gio. An accident I could see, but premeditated murder? I swallowed hard.

"Worked out for me, too," Ryan said. His mother cleared her throat, and he shot her an apologetic look. "Well, almost."

I cocked my head to the side. "What do you mean?"

He held up his broken arm. "Needed Adam to come rescue me that morning."

"What happened?"

He glanced up at his mom, his expression unchanged from before. "I snuck out to go to the skate park. Tried to do this wicked trick and came down wrong. Broke my board and my arm. Called Adam because I wasn't gonna call Mom."

Relief flooded my system as I searched Adam's face. "So you went and rescued your brother?"

Adam nodded. "Had to convince him to go see a doctor. He didn't want to."

His brother shrugged. "She never would have found out if I hadn't gotten hurt."

"I hated that board," their mom confessed. "Good riddance."

"I'm getting another board, Mom," Ryan said as if it were a done deal.

Adam snorted. "Yeah, one that's properly sized for you, not something you used in high school when you were still short and Dad was threatening to throw you back into the water with the rest of the lobsters that were too small. Some new gloves too." He shook his head. "Can't believe you lost yours."

"Wouldn't have helped with my arm."

Adam sputtered. "It could have helped your grip to prevent it from happening."

Their mom made a face. "Well, you're not getting *anything* for another six weeks. And then you need to save up for it all." She made it sound as if that might take a while.

"Mom . . ." Ryan groaned.

"Don't *mom* me. Now come on, boys. Let's go pay our respects." She turned her younger son using his good arm and marched him to the line.

Adam smiled at me apologetically. "She's not happy with either of us right now. She knows I wouldn't have told her if he hadn't been that hurt."

"You're a good big brother." And thankfully not a killer. But who was?

CHAPTER TWENTY-SEVEN

The room fell into a hush as Adam joined his mom and brother. I glanced at the front of the room, expecting one of the Underhills to be standing there, ready to tell us to take our seats for Gio's funeral service. But the Underhills were nowhere in sight and Gio's family was still in line, greeting people and thanking them for coming.

The grandfather clock ticking in the corner indicated there was still a half hour left before the service would begin. So why the silence?

I turned toward the entrance in time to see Naomi and Floyd walking in together.

At that moment, I was glad Naomi had Floyd. I couldn't imagine having to walk into an ex-husband's funeral alone. Naomi had said she'd been getting flowers weekly from Gio up until she and Floyd got together, so clearly Gio still had feelings for her, but did his family know that? I had friends whose parents had split amicably, but I'd seen divorces not go so well too.

Naomi's eyes were glassy as she surveyed the room, and I

smiled warmly at her from my spot a few feet away where I'd been talking to Adam and his family. She returned the gesture, only the look was hesitant, her lips barely curling upward. Then she sucked in a breath and held it, pulling her arm from Floyd's and steeling herself.

Heavy footfalls sounded, and I barely had time to register Gina passing me before she'd enveloped Naomi in a huge hug. Her head blocked me from seeing Naomi's face, but Naomi pulled Gina even closer. She slid her arms under Gina's and locked up behind her shoulders. A sob escaped one of them— or maybe both—as they swayed in their embrace.

Once again, I had to wipe my eyes. It didn't surprise me that Gina would be the one to go to Naomi, not after the summer she spent here. I would imagine that made them closer than others in the family. But I was glad to see them hug as opposed to the opposite. Gina's reaction seemed to break everyone else out of their hush. It was as if they'd all been waiting to see what would happen, and now that the moment had passed, they were free to talk again.

After a moment, the two women let each other go, and Naomi reached into her bag for tissues. Both needed one. Then, leaning on one another, they walked arm in arm to the front of the line, passing the remaining few still needing to pay their respects.

Floyd remained in the entrance, his face tight, looking unsure of what to do. I couldn't imagine being in his position either. The new man at the funeral of the ex. I doubted he'd have come to Gio's funeral if he wasn't doing it to support Naomi.

We were a small town, and while everyone knew of everyone else, it wasn't like the whole town showed up at these sorts of things. Though with Gio and Flour Power's popularity, this one was well attended. No one who should have been here was missing, though. That would have been my sign of guilt. Statistics showed victims were more likely to know their murderer. It was why they always looked at family first. So either the killer was here and hiding their guilt well, or the person who killed Gio hadn't been close to him.

"Can I please have your attention?" Mr. Underhill asked from the podium at the front corner of the room next to the line of Gio's family. "The service will begin momentarily. Please find your seats so we may begin."

Floyd sat in an unoccupied chair in the back corner of the arranged seats, and I made my way to an open spot between my mother and Mrs. Roland. Dad was now sitting on the other side of Mom.

She pulled her purse off the free chair as I approached. "I meant to ask you," she began once I sat down, "Why is Trouble outside?"

"Trouble's outside?" I repeated as if that were news to me. "He's a cat. I don't know what he does when he leaves the house."

She eyed me. "While wearing a bow tie?"

I shrugged. "I put him in it this morning. Cute, isn't it?"

"Very, but it almost seems as if he's dressed up for a funeral."

I blew a short raspberry. "He didn't even know Gio."

My attempt at being funny didn't have the effect I was going for. Mom said nothing but continued to study me, her lips tight in a straight line.

"Mom, I repeat, Trouble is a cat. He probably followed me here. It's not like I told him to meet me. It's a miracle that he lets me put his collar on."

"You don't seem very concerned about him being out there."

"Gio's funeral is about to start. I'm not going to run out of here to go bring him home. He found a way here, and he can find the same way back." She didn't need to know that his way here and back was my car.

When the funeral was over, I stayed chatting with people as long as possible, outlasting my parents so I could grab Trubbs and go home. That was if he'd stayed through the service. He'd done his job scoping out people as they got to the funeral home. I could see him going off somewhere once he realized more weren't coming.

Understandably, Gio's family was among the last to leave as well, including Naomi. I went up to them once more to express my condolences and tell Gina how good it was to see her despite the circumstances. I owed Heartwood Hollow a visit after this. Trubbs would probably enjoy the trip too. Especially once I told him that Joanie had been the one to send me the recipe to make his cat treats.

After Gio's family said their goodbyes and left to speak with the Underhills, I put my hand on Naomi's forearm. "How are you doing?"

She let out a soft sigh. "Okay, I guess. That went better than expected. Thank goodness for Gina. I wasn't sure I'd be able to go up to them."

"Even with Floyd?"

Naomi nodded. "Especially with Floyd, actually. Have you seen him?" She looked around me at all the seats.

I turned to follow her gaze. "He'd sat right in the back, there," I said, pointing. "Why didn't he sit with you?"

She tapped my hand, and we began walking to the door. "He must be out in the car. To answer your question, I told him he didn't have to. I didn't want to force Gio's family to sit with the man I chose over their son and brother. And I didn't want Floyd to do anything that would make him uncomfortable. Being the other man—not that he was the other man like that, mind you, Gio and I were already long divorced—but making him sit with Gio's grieving family? No, I couldn't do that to him. Floyd being here was enough."

"I see," I said, grabbing the front door for her. The Under-hills were likely all talking with Gio's family. Muted voices came from behind the office door.

"Are you coming to the lunch?" Naomi asked as we stepped outside. "It's nothing formal since his family will be going back home this evening. They'll do something for Gio there too."

"I don't want to insert myself," I replied, glancing around for Trubbs. He was nowhere near the entrance as we let the door close behind us and then followed the path around the building. I wasn't surprised by his absence.

Naomi shook her head. "You wouldn't be. You'd be my plus one. And really, I should have thought about asking everyone from the bakery to come. You all knew him best."

But not well enough to know who might have wanted him dead, but I wasn't going to say that. "What about Floyd?"

"He has leftover pizza to eat. Thank you for that, by the way. I'm glad you ran into him. It was nice to have something other than my butterless and cheeseless bread."

"Yeah, about that. I didn't realize you baked. You were never in the kitchen at Flour Power."

She smiled warmly. "Not there, no. But I did all the baking at home so Gio didn't have to. When we didn't just take things home from the bakery, of course."

"I had no idea."

"Mm-hmm. The kitchen was always Gio's domain. He could work the shop, sure, but too many people exhausted him."

"Is that why you're interested in getting the bakery back?"

She cocked her head to the side. "Who told you that?"

"Floyd mentioned it. Said you were having your lawyers look into it."

She nodded. "I wanted to make sure there was nothing on my end tying me to any debts he might have had or anything like that." That didn't sound like a motive for murder to me. The opposite, if anything. "But I'd be lying if I said I wasn't interested now. We developed a lot of the recipes we brought to Flour Power together. Some of them were my sole creations."

Her admission caused me to stop dead in my tracks. "That's why he didn't want to change things."

She'd taken a step or two without me and now had to turn back to look at me. "Come again?"

"The recipes. He wouldn't change them."

"Oh," she said on an exhale, waiting for me to catch up with her before walking again.

"It's why I was fired actually," I said, wanting to change the subject so she couldn't dwell on what that could mean.

"You were fired?" Her mouth hung partially open.

"You didn't know? I could have sworn I'd brought it up."

She shrugged, her mouth closing. "You might have. Things have been foggy the last couple days. You can tell me about it over lunch."

We reached the parking lot, and there was Trubbs, waiting on top of my car.

"I thought you'd never get here. I'm hungry," he complained with an audible meow.

"Oh," Naomi squealed. "There's that adorable cat."

"That's Trouble. My cat."

"What's he doing here?"

"He likes to go for rides," I stated as if it were no big deal.

Trubbs jumped from my car to the pavement. He trotted

over to us and rubbed around Naomi's legs. "That will show that fat cat of hers."

I sucked in a portion of my lower lip to keep from laughing.

Naomi squatted down and pet Trubbs, cooing over every headbutt he gave her. "Spatch is going to hate this, but how can you not pet such a sweet cat? And that bow tie!"

"Isn't he handsome?" I agreed.

Trubbs headbutted her leg. "That's right, handsome and hungry."

"So about lunch," I began, "Do you want to meet me? Or if you want, I can drive."

Still scratching Trouble's neck, Naomi glanced up at me. "You wouldn't mind?"

"Not at all. It's Wisteria Falls. Your house will take me all of a minute out of my way when lunch is over. It's no big deal."

"What about your cat? Shouldn't you take him home?"

Trubbs meowed and headbutted her again. "I will head to Robin's house and grab something with the other cats. I'll be fine."

"He's good. Like Spatch, he kinda does what he wants. He knows where to go from here."

"I can't believe you just compared me to that cat." He walked away from Naomi and wound around my legs. "But I'll allow it given the company."

He'd forgive me later once I gave him a treat.

"Well, if you're sure . . . Let me go tell Floyd." She crossed the parking lot toward Floyd's car.

I bent down and undid Trouble's collar. "Sorry about that," I whispered. "You sure you're okay going to Robin's?"

"Sure I am. She likes me." Of course the cat lady liked him. She probably liked Spatch too, but I wasn't going to tell him that. Trubbs headbutted me. "Lots of cat owners, by the way, but no one was furry enough to identify suspects by fur. Sorry to say I'm not sure if your killer was here."

I sighed. "It's okay. It was a long shot anyway." They probably kept their good clothes away from their cats like I did (or tried to). "Thanks for trying. See you at home later."

Trubbs trotted off toward the far side of the parking lot, and I shoved his collar into my purse. Thank goodness for that microchip.

"Ready to go?" Naomi asked as I was standing back up. I hadn't heard her approach.

"Sure am."

"Great. Now you can tell me more about getting fired."

Chapter Twenty-Eight

Trubbs was waiting for me back at my apartment when I got home from dropping off Naomi after lunch. He'd startled me enough that I jumped back, hitting the door with my backside and slamming it shut. I'd have probably tripped over him if that hadn't happened. He was that close to the door.

I immediately went to the refrigerator and grabbed him a lobster treat, one hand still on my chest as my heart calmed. "Here you go, Trubb's. You earned it. Did you get enough lunch at Robin's?"

He didn't answer me until he was done with the treat. "Not quite," he admitted.

But I was already one step ahead of him and grabbing out his cat food. He'd said before that he always ate last so the strays could get their fill.

"I figured based on the way you scarfed that down. Did you even taste it?" I should have given him some of the treats from the pet store so he could have savored the lobster one later. "We're running low, just to let you know. It'll be a while before I get lobster again, although I'm happy to report that the guy who sold it to me wasn't Gio's killer."

"That's good." He barely waited for me to finish pouring crunchies into his bowl before diving in. Between bites, he asked, "So when are we going to this garden place you keep telling me about?"

"That's right." I'd forgotten all about it with everything going on and really hadn't had the time since I'd gone by myself. "We'll go soon, I promise. I need to get another blog post with you in it up on my blog soon."

In truth, Wisteria Falls was the best place to take him right now. It was a nice, easy trip to get used to his harness and to staying with me while we walked. Plus, with the gardens being free for all Wisteria Falls residents, it fit within my budget. I wasn't going anywhere until Gio's killer was behind bars, not that I had the money for travel right now. Between getting Trubbs and using him as an excuse for a bit of retail therapy after Gio's death, this was going to be a tight month for my wallet. I'd have to check with Mrs. Roland tomorrow to see if she needed me to continue working at the floral shop.

While Trouble continued to eat, I changed out of my clothes and then settled into my recliner, grabbing my laptop to work on my blog. Readers were already commenting on my first post about Trubbs. They needed to see more photos of him. The few pictures I'd posted of him on social media had more likes than many of my others did too. I should have thought to take a picture of him in his bowtie this morning. We'd have to do that some other time.

No doubt rebranding to Purrfect Travel Companion had been a good move. After just the one post introducing him, I'd gained fifteen new followers. Few, if any, of my previous followers seemed to mind the change, likely because the core of my blog was still about travel. The places I visited, the things I did, and the food I ate. Now it had a cat who would do all those things with me as often as I could take him places. I was sure I'd still have to have some solo travels.

But first I had to finish these posts about my recent overnight in Saltair Shores. I'd skipped to the end about getting Trubbs and talking about Feline Familiar Cat Café in Snowhaven. Maybe I'd talk about the candy I'd bought at the country store down there first. Or my amazing Italian dinner. Eventually, I'd have to write about my visit to the bakery there, where I'd been given a behind-the-scenes tour. I'd told the owners I'd let them know when it was live, so I knew they were waiting, but I wasn't ready to talk about someone else's bakery.

Ten minutes (and what felt like forever) later, I'd been sitting here that whole time without putting a word onto the page.

Without a doubt, even though I'd warned people that the next few posts wouldn't include Trouble, they'd be asking where he was. Might as well give them what they want.

"Trubbs, you want to take a selfie?"

Finished with his lunch, he scrambled up behind me on the recliner. "What is a selfie?" He leaned forward, placing his front paws on my shoulder.

"Don't move." I carefully slid my phone out of my back pocket. No easy feat while sitting on it and trying not to throw Trubbs off balance. With my phone successfully retrieved, I held my arm out and faced the screen toward us with the camera on. "This is a selfie." *Click*.

Trubbs was a natural. I knew he would be based on his reaction at the pet store with his collar. Once he understood I was taking pictures, not just letting him see himself, he even posed.

Click. Click. Click.

And then he slipped. *Thunk.*

"You okay?" I asked, grabbing my shoulder.

Trubbs looked up at me from the floor. "All good. What about you?"

"I think it's time to clip your nails, but I'll live."

He glared at me.

I put one hand up in surrender while the other held my laptop steady. Thank goodness it hadn't fallen with Trubbs. "Not right now. That's going to require another trip to the pet store. Besides, it's probably best that you have them since you insist on going outside without me."

Trubbs jumped onto the recliner once more and then settled in his usual spot between my head and the backrest. Together we stayed that way until I'd finally finished a blog post. Two, actually. It had taken longer than I'd have liked, but once I'd written about Trubbs, a post about the Italian dinner I'd eaten had come easily. Eventually I would have to face the bakery post, but not today. And despite having a sizeable lunch with Gio's family and Naomi, writing my posts had made me hungry too. Posting food photos and writing about them was dangerous like that.

"Okay, Trubbs. Just let me put up one photo of us on social media to announce my latest blog post and I'll be all set."

He stretched and maneuvered himself so he could plop his head over my shoulder. "I want to see."

I switched to the other tab in my browser window and brought up the selfies we'd taken. "Have a preference?"

"Do NOT use that one." He could only mean the one of him falling off me.

I snorted. "But it's funny." Though I didn't look much better than he did with his claws digging into me as I snapped the photo. I'd have to save it for a throwback post on social media someday. Or a blooper reel if we ever got famous.

"I'm serious. Use the one over there." I highlighted the one I thought he meant. "No, next to it. Yes."

His head was tilted against mine in this one. "I like it." I loaded it to my social media manager and quickly drafted a post that would send out on all my socials. "And done."

Trouble slipped down to the floor, this time purposely and without claws. "Good. Now can I have a snack? Your stomach started rumbling halfway through your work, and now I'm hungry."

I closed my laptop and put it on the side table next to me. "You're always hungry."

"Yes, but now I need you to do something about it." He trotted over to his metal food bowl. "It's empty."

As I stood up to get him a snack, my cell phone rang. I grabbed it off the arm of the recliner and glanced at the screen.

The Wisteria Falls Police Department.

Chapter Twenty-Nine

I slid my thumb up the screen to accept the call. "Hello?"

"Mer?"

"Jay." Thank goodness it was him calling and not Owens. "Or should I be calling you Officer Roland while you're at work?"

Amusement laced his voice as he said, "Jay's fine."

"Okay, but you are calling from the station, so this is an official call. What's up?"

"If you could come down to the station whenever's convenient, that would be great."

My heart did a weird stutter stop in the half second before I asked why. Trubbs, still waiting at his empty dish, tilted his head as he looked at me.

"Your shoes are back. You can come get them."

"Does this mean I'm no longer a suspect?"

A hard rush of air escaped him. "Yeah, no. Your feet are way too small."

"My feet aren't tiny either, so those have to have been some pretty big shoes." An invisible weight lifted off me.

Although I knew I'd done nothing, having that be the official stance of the WFPD as well, made me feel tons better.

"Shoot. I probably shouldn't have said that. Mer, strike that from your head and do not tell Rita. We don't want this getting out to the public."

"I think you're going to have a harder time not telling Rita than I am. You already told me the cat fur you found doesn't match Trubbs's fur. And no. I haven't told your sister about that either."

He chuckled. "If I remember correctly, I only told you they didn't match. I said nothing about *how*."

"You got me there." Would have been helpful had he let that tidbit slip. "How much longer are you going to be at the station?"

"A while. Just got here."

"Okay. I'll be down in a bit. Gotta feed Trubbs."

"About time," Trubbs called from the kitchen.

Ignoring him as I crossed the living room, I continued, "He's staring at me like I'm starving him. For the record, I'm not."

"I never thought you were. I guess I will see you soon, then." He cleared his throat and took on a more official tone as he said, "You can ask Dennis at the desk to page me, and I'll walk them down for you."

"Such personal attention," I teased.

"It's . . . part of my job," he replied, seemingly flustered.

"See you soon, Jay." I clicked *end* on my screen and opened up the cupboard where Trubbs's food was. "Sorry about that, Trubbs," I started and then filled him in on what Jay had revealed.

"Too bad I wasn't paying attention to the size of peoples' shoes, only if there was cat fur on them."

"Well, it tells us we can probably rule out a vast majority

of women in Wisteria Falls. At least half the men too. My feet are a size nine and a half." I held my foot up for his inspection. "That's bigger than the norm. It only makes me an eight in men's shoes, though, which is slightly smaller than average." The things you learned during college trivia nights.

"I'll keep an eye out, but I try to stay away from people's feet. The other day was an exception. I hate when my tail gets stepped on." He flicked it for good measure. "Food now?"

"Oh, right. Sorry." I poured him some more food, perhaps a half serving as compared to a regular meal. Then I put on a pair of flats, grabbed my bag, and left the apartment.

A few minutes later, I was at the station. Compared to two days before, the building was quieter. The reporters were gone. Most had cleared out that first evening. Whether it was her decision or the station's, Rita's ten-minute taped interview with me had gotten cut to a thirty-second sound bite. But it had made me sound uninteresting enough that none of the other regional news outlets had contacted me, which was fine by me.

"Hey Meredith," Dennis said from the desk as he typed something into the computer.

I smiled at the older man. He was one of my dad's friends. In this small town, nearly everyone was a friend of his. As one of two mail carriers for the town, Dad knew everyone. All the dogs too. Too bad he probably didn't know all the cats, not that I knew what type of cat to look for.

"Afternoon, Dennis. I'm here to grab my shoes back from Jason."

He cracked a smile. "Left your shoes, huh?"

"Not like that." Although I knew he was joking, heat rose into my cheeks all the same. "They were evidence."

"Oh, I was just teasing. Trying to get you to smile, that's all." He inclined his head toward me. "Looks like I did my job. But are you sweet on Officer Roland? What's your dad think?"

"Dennis . . ." I groaned.

"All right, all right." He chuckled. "Let me buzz him."

Dennis pressed a button on the phone as he picked up the receiver. "Yeah, Jay, I have a Miss Duffy here to collect her shoes. Great, I'll let her know." He put the handset back on the cradle, then pulled a sheet of paper from a drawer in the desk. "Jay asked me to get you started on this. He'll be out in a minute."

"Ah. This will be easy enough," I said as Dennis slid the paper across the desktop. "I've already had to do one of these for my paycheck."

His usual goofy grin fell. "I hate that you had to go through this. Sorry about Gio. Shame what happened."

"It is," I agreed and grabbed a pen from the holder sitting a foot away on the desk. He said nothing more, and I didn't either as I filled out the chain of custody form to say that I was getting my shoes back. A day in a fancy pair for Gio's funeral and then putting on my flats to come down here had confirmed I was a sneakers kind of girl. And even those had been partially ruined for me by this pair of work shoes. They were plain and not all that attractive, but they were so comfortable they'd become my regular walking shoes. I wore them when I traveled too.

"Mer, thanks for coming by." I clicked my pen and looked up to see Jay holding my shoes. "It's good to see you."

Since we had an audience, who would no doubt tell my dad about this innocent encounter during their next poker night, I looked at Jay directly as I took the bag with my sneakers from him. "It's good to see these. You too, Jay." I winked at him.

Dennis snorted. "She's quick, Jay. You better watch your-self with this one."

"Oh, I know. I've been chasing her for years." Jay gazed at me intently, blue eyes twinkling.

I fought to keep my mouth from dropping open. What was I supposed to say to something like that? If that wasn't a declaration of his interest, nothing was. How had I been so oblivious to it?

"Thank you for these," I finally said and swallowed hard. Was it warm in here or was it just me?

Dennis chuckled, breaking the moment. So much for not giving him something to talk about. Somehow my attempt at a joke had given him way more to tell my dad than I had intended.

"Welcome," Jay started. "Sorry we had to collect them from you at all. I know you'd never do anything to Gio."

Dennis sputtered. "We *all* know that."

Except for Owens, but I wasn't going to remind them. I didn't want to make things awkward between Jay and his new partner.

Jay tapped the desk. "I'm going to walk Mer back to her car in case anyone asks where I am."

"Roger that." Dennis turned to me. "You have a good rest of your day and behave yourself." His gaze had darted up to Jay with the last part of that sentence.

"Always do." Or at least I tried.

Jay led me out of the station and out onto the sidewalk next to my car. There'd been plenty of room to park, and it was past the time of day when I had to worry about the posted time limit on the sign.

"So about that coffee," Jay began.

"I thought we were going to wait until you found Gio's killer." Not that I wanted to wait anymore.

He shook his head, a smile creeping across his face. "No, *you* said we should wait until after that. But we'd agreed it wouldn't look good if I was taking a suspect in his murder out for coffee."

"And I'm no longer a suspect." My smile now matched his.

"So I was wondering if you'd reconsider the order of things. It's still an active investigation, of course, but we're out of immediate leads." He rubbed the back of his neck. It was cute how nervous he was about this. "I don't know how long it could go on for, and I really don't want to wait to take you out, so I was hoping . . ."

"That we could grab that coffee?"

"Or maybe dinner?" He lowered his arm.

"Like a proper date?"

He shrugged, cocking his head slightly to the side. "If you wanted it to be."

"Oh, I do." More than I thought I did even a few minutes ago.

"Great. I'm on nights until Wednesday, so Wednesday night?"

"I'd like that."

"It's settled, then. Wednesday night. You wanna pick the place?"

I shook my head. "Something tells me you've thought about this already and probably have a place in mind. I trust you."

Jay stumbled over his next words. "Okay. It's a date." He took a step toward me, and I instinctively moved forward to hug him the way I had dozens of times before over the years. Then he seemed to think better of it, and he rubbed the back of his neck again. "I should probably get back inside."

"Okay," I said in a voice pitched higher than usual, my heartbeat thumping erratically. Slightly embarrassed, I realized something had shifted between us. He had to have sensed it too. "See you Wednesday."

I watched Jay walk back into the station before getting into my car. That uniform made him look good. Then before I started the engine, I connected my phone to the car's Bluetooth system so I could talk through the speakers while I drove.

Rita had to hear about this.

CHAPTER THIRTY

Except I didn't end up calling Rita.

"Hello?" Came the voice on the other end of the line.

When I heard Mrs. Roland's voice, it took me a split second to realize what I'd done and unfreeze from being caught off guard by not hearing Rita answer. Thank goodness I hadn't already been driving.

Still flustered by the exchange with Jay, I'd told my phone to call not Rita Evans, her married name, but Rita Roland, the name she'd grown up with and kept for TV because she liked the sound of it.

Rita Roland, however, still existed in my contacts list, but it went to her parents' house.

I took a steadying breath as I pulled away from the curb in front of the station. "Hi, Mrs. Roland. It's Meredith."

"Oh, Meredith, I was just thinking about you." Unless Jay had texted his mom to say we were going on a date, there was no way she knew what had transpired moments before. "I gave Floyd the next two days off to help Naomi with whatever she might need. Think you might be interested in giving me a hand?"

"Absolutely." I'd intended to ask her anyway.

"It would just be the two days for now. We're closed Wednesdays unless there's a special need, but let's hope no one else in this town dies before then."

"I'm happy to help as long as needed. Don't worry about it."

"You're a lifesaver. Thank you so much. So I'll see you tomorrow?"

"Sounds good. See you tomorrow."

Before either of us disconnected, Mrs. Roland called my name as if she remembered something as she was going to hang up their landline. "Meredith?"

"What's up, Mrs. Roland?"

"Why were you calling?"

I swallowed a chuckle. Confessing that I'd accidentally called her and not Rita might have resulted in me admitting the why as well. "Same reason you wanted to talk to me, actually." It wasn't really a lie. It just wasn't planned for that moment.

"What a coincidence. You have a good evening."

"You too," I replied as I pulled into my driveway.

Once I was inside my apartment, I texted Rita to call me when she could, to make sure I didn't call her mom by mistake for a second time.

Working in a flower shop was a lot like working in the front half of the bakery. I greeted customers, got them what they wanted, and rung them out. Mrs. Roland made most of the arrangements. I was happy to make two of the smaller ones following her book of instructions.

Although I'd been on edge all day, scrutinizing the customers with a smile on my face as I wondered if they could be Gio's killer, Monday came and went without incident. It was easy to rule the customers out after a glance or two.

It was my second morning there when the bell above the door chimed as Floyd walked in, broken flowers in hand. I recognized them. They were the same as the ones I'd delivered to Naomi the other day. But the flowers weren't the only thing I noticed. I'd never paid attention before, never had a reason to before now.

Floyd had humongous feet.

"Floyd, what happened? Mrs. Roland asked as she came out of one of the refrigerated rooms where she kept the cut flowers unless she was working with them.

Floyd set the banged-up flowers on the counter between him and me. "Naomi's cat had a bit of a run-in with the vase of flowers that she got from you on Saturday. These are the best-looking ones left out of the bunch. The vase completely shattered."

Mrs. Roland placed a hand over her heart. "Oh, poor Naomi."

"Yeah, it hasn't made things any easier for her."

"Was Spatch okay?" I asked, my gaze going past the flowers on the counter to Floyd's fur-speckled shirt. If only I knew what kind of cat fur had been found on Gio's body. This was about as different from Trubbs's as it got.

Floyd seemed thrown off a moment. "Spatch?"

"Yeah, with the glass."

"Oh." Floyd chuckled. "Took off like a rocket. I think he was feet away by the time the vase hit the ground."

"That's good. He's so furry it might be hard to tell if he got a cut."

"Is there any way I could get a replacement for these? I'll pay, of course."

I forced my gaze away from his shirt and to Mrs. Roland. "Do we have any more of these yellow ones?" I couldn't recall the name.

She frowned. "I think we used the last ones in the arrangements we did for Gio." Mrs. Roland turned her attention back to Floyd. "We could make her something close. A new batch of those flowers is due in on Friday, so she'll get a fresh bunch then."

Floyd's brows furrowed. "Who's going to send them to her?"

"Gio is. Same as before."

"But Gio's dead," he stated flatly.

"And he paid in advance, so she'll continue to get flowers for as long as there's money in the account he had with me. Really, Floyd, after all this time, I thought you knew."

Wait, so Gio had been sending Naomi flowers all along? Naomi had acted like the bouquet I gave her was the first one in quite some time. Even mentioned it being nice that Mrs. Roland had thought to send them. Had she been making it up? Covering for her boyfriend perhaps?

No, I'd seen her at the funeral with Gina. She couldn't have faked those emotions.

So if she'd not gotten flowers until I delivered them the other day, what had Floyd been doing with them?

He shrugged slowly, seemingly disappointed. "Guess I just assumed they would stop."

Was that it? He'd gotten tired of having to fake deliver flowers to his girlfriend from her ex-husband? I could see how that was annoying, but he'd been doing it for a year. What had changed that would turn it into a motive for murder?

"There are several more months' worth in his account."

"Maybe you could start doing biweekly or even monthly bouquets instead," I suggested. "Your flowers last way longer than a week anyway."

Floyd's eyes widened. My guess was he didn't like the idea of having to deal with Gio's flowers for any longer than he had to. Even if he wasn't bringing them to Naomi.

Mrs. Roland considered this a moment. "Oh, I'd hate to change the agreement I'd had with Gio, but you're right. I bet she gets overrun with them after a while. She did tell me early on that she had enough vases."

"One less now," I commented. Had Spatch even knocked them over, or had Floyd done something to them and blamed the cat?

"Yes, well, that I can fix. Let's get a new bouquet done up so you can get it back to Naomi." She waved for Floyd to follow her into the back room. No doubt he'd made this bouquet dozens of times and could help come up with alternatives for it. At least he'd have to give this one to Naomi.

Once they were far enough back that they couldn't see me through the glass walls of the refrigerated room, I pulled my phone from my bag under the desk. I had to text Jay and hoped it was early enough that he wouldn't be at work yet.

Me: Did you ever look into Floyd as a suspect?

After a moment, nothing. Maybe he was annoyed that I was involving myself again.

Me: I promise I'm not investigating on my own, but I saw his shoes today, and they are huge. He has a cat, too.

Still nothing. By the time I saw Mrs. Roland and Floyd coming back toward the main part of the shop a few minutes later, I had yet to receive a reply. But I couldn't keep checking my phone, so I slid it into my bag.

Unfortunately, I was a little too slow.

"As Rita and Jay used to say to one another," Mrs. Roland began, "Busted."

"Sorry. I was just checking real quick."

"Checking a flower ID app, perhaps?" She grinned knowingly.

I shook my head. I'd never been able to lie to Mrs. Roland, not outright and not to her face, though the flower app sounded like a good idea if I ended up here regularly.

"So who were you hoping to see a text from that it couldn't wait?"

Even on the phone yesterday, I'd come close to spilling the real reason I'd called. Now, yesterday's secret would save me from spilling today's.

"Jay." My face flushed. Although I'd been wanting to talk to him for another reason, my face had other ideas when it came to mentioning him to his mom.

"Ah . . ." she said, dragging out the sound, her smile widening.

There was only one reason she'd be making that face. "You know, don't you?"

"He may have mentioned it yesterday morning when I saw him. And again this morning. We have breakfast together when he works nights. I have it ready for him when he gets home, so he doesn't have to spend the time making something and can go to bed when he's done."

"That's sweet of you."

She dismissed the comment with a wave. "It lets me know he's at least eating something. He may be all grown now, but a mother still worries about their kids getting enough to eat when they live on their own." Not that staying in the in-law apartment attached to his house was completely like living alone, though I didn't judge since my situation was the same.

My initial embarrassment of getting caught peeking at the phone and the resulting admission about my upcoming date—even if it wasn't the real reason I was looking at my phone—had momentarily made me forget Floyd was still there until he finally excused himself.

"I should get these back to Naomi. She's probably wondering about me." He lifted the new bouquet in a brand-new vase. "Thank you."

Without hearing back from Jay, there was nothing I could do or say to keep Floyd here for as long as I possibly needed him to be. And as much as I had suspicion, I didn't have proof. And if he was guilty and I did something now to tip him off, I couldn't prevent him from leaving town completely. At least by letting him go, I knew he was going back home.

"Give my best to Naomi," Mrs. Roland said. "Do let her know that if she needs anything to not hesitate to call."

Floyd nodded. "I will, thanks. See you Thursday." As he passed me on his way out, he said, "Good luck with your date. About time."

Even Floyd knew? He and Jay had been friends in high school when Floyd first moved here, but despite our small town, they hadn't remained close after graduation.

"Thanks." I gave him an awkward smile. What else was I supposed to say to that? Especially given what I suspected of him.

"For what it's worth," Mrs. Roland began once we were alone, "I approve of you going on a date with Jay. As Floyd said, it's about time."

Heat flared in my cheeks, and my smile turned shy but

genuine as I averted my gaze. Suddenly, I couldn't look the woman who I'd known nearly as long as my own mom in the face. "I had no idea," I finally admitted.

"And why would you have? I think it took a while for him to admit to himself." She chuckled. "Everyone else had it figured out long before you two did."

"Thanks, that makes me feel less, I don't know, guilty over being so oblivious."

She placed her hand on my arm. "Aww, now, it's all right. Not like he's had the nerve to ask you until now. But let's get back to work, shall we? You won't hear from him for a while still."

I cocked my head to the side. Was he working a lead? "Oh? Why's that?"

"He's still sleeping after his night shift."

"Oh, right." Whoops. "I hope I didn't wake him up with my text earlier."

She barked out a laugh. "There is no way a text woke up my son. He sleeps like a rock when he's off duty. Not even the foghorn on the lighthouse woke him up as a baby."

Everyone in Wisteria Falls could hear the foghorn on nights when it was needed, but the Rolands lived in one of the houses closest to the beautiful light, and therefore they heard it the loudest. After one terrible night sleeping over as a kid while it blared all night in a soupy fog, I had Mom check the weather before I'd agree to stay there. If the weather seemed less than optimal, I would invite Rita over instead.

"Well, whatever you texted him," Mrs. Roland continued, "I'm sure it will put a smile on his face when he wakes up and sees it."

If only she knew what I'd sent. I doubted she'd be happy to read it either. She'd feel terrible thinking there was a possibility that Floyd had killed Gio.

"I hope so." And for the rest of the day, all I could hope was that there'd be a text waiting for me when I got done with work.

CHAPTER THIRTY-ONE

Although Mrs. Roland told me I could take off as she cashed out the register for the evening, I dragged my feet getting ready, part wanting to see if she'd say anything about my coming back to work again on Thursday, but she'd said nothing.

Right now, at least, she still had Floyd.

My stall tactics meant we left together. She sighed as she stopped and locked the door behind us. "I've been extra vigilant in doing this since Gio's death. Can't be too careful."

"I'm sure Davis appreciates it," I quipped.

She chuckled at the mention of her insurance agent. "You have a good night, Meredith, and thank you again for helping me today."

"You got it, Mrs. Roland."

"And have fun tomorrow." Gone was any worry she'd momentarily had over locking the shop. Now she stood smirking at me, her eyes darting to my bag where my phone sat at the top. But I wasn't going to check it with her right there. I couldn't. It would have been too weird.

"Thanks. I'm looking forward to it." Before heat could rise any further up my cheeks, I turned and strolled away from her, doing my best to be nonchalant. My hand itched to reach into my bag and grab my phone. It was almost as if I could feel her staring, waiting for me to pull it out to look at it.

As soon as I'd turned the corner, putting me out of Mrs. Roland's view, I yanked my phone out of my bag.

Jay: Of course we looked into him. He was the third person we considered. He has an alibi.

The first two, I knew, were me and Naomi. But I still had my doubts about Floyd.

Me: Is it a good alibi? Did you know about his big feet when you first looked into him?

Jay: Yes, and that cat too. Unless you have something more substantial that destroys his alibi, it's not him. Do you really think that I'd not look into him fully when he works for my mom?

I worried that I'd annoyed him. He'd told me to stay out of it, and here I was definitely in it. I sighed.

Me: You're right. Guess I freaked out a little bit when he came into your mom's shop today and I saw his shoes. Sorry.

Jay: It's okay. I know you cared for Gio and want to see this solved. We're working on it.

And I knew that. But how many suspects could there be? If not Floyd, then who?

Me: I hope I didn't wake you up.

Jay: Nope. Put a smile on my face when I saw your name. I'm looking forward to our date tomorrow.

Nice of him to avoid saying he stopped smiling when he read my text.

Me: I am too. Have a good night at work. See you tomorrow!

Now tomorrow was here, and I paced the floor of my bedroom as I stared at my open closet figuring out what to wear. I had hours still, but I wanted to be prepared. And to hide whatever outfit I decided on as soon as possible to minimize the amount of fur on it.

"If you don't pick something soon," Trubbs commented from the bed, "you're not going to want to go to the garden with me."

"What do you mean?" I pulled out a blue blouse and immediately shoved it back into the closet.

He nodded toward my feet. "You'll have done too much walking in that three-foot space."

I stopped in my tracks. "Sorry. I didn't realize how nervous I'd get. It's just Jay, right? This should be easy. I've known him forever."

Trubbs flicked his tail. "But the way you're seeing him now is different. As I heard many people at the cat café say, he obviously likes you. All the signs are there."

"You picked up a lot at that café. Genetics, relationship advice, what else do you know?"

"Plenty." I swore he smiled. "People of all kinds went there. I learned a lot."

"Any of it pertain to clothes? I have no idea what to wear." I couldn't believe I was asking a cat for fashion advice.

"Go with the green one."

I grabbed the green sundress and held it to my body. It still had the tags on it. "You think?"

"Yeah. It reminds me of my collar."

I pulled the tag off. It wasn't like I had a better reason to wear it or anything else in my closet. "Green dress it is." Then I took the dress and, after giving it a quick go-over with the lint roller, slung it over the bar on the back of the bathroom door, hoping it was too high for Trubbs's fur to reach. Back in the closet wasn't an option. Its door was no match for this cat. I'd already found him in there once.

"Great! Now let's go to the garden."

Chapter Thirty-Two

"You know I can slip out of it if I want to, right?" Trubbs said as I got him into his harness. "It's not much harder than a collar. At least for me."

I crossed my arms and stared at him still sitting on the front passenger seat. "You can't go running off. You promised."

"And *you* promised we could try going off leash if I stayed with you. You never know when there might be a reason for me to not be attached to you at all times on these trips."

"I know, but we also talked about how some places won't allow that. There's a leash law here, which means you need to stay on a leash." I pulled ours from a pocket on my small travel backpack and clipped it to the harness.

"There's a rule that *dogs* need to stay on a leash here," he corrected.

"I'm sure it doesn't say *only* dogs. Though that's probably the assumption. I don't imagine that they get many cats coming to the botanical gardens to feel like they have to specify. Come on. You do good here, and next time I'll take you somewhere that doesn't require a leash the whole time."

"Deal."

After double-checking to make sure Trubbs was secure in his harness, I slung my camera around my neck, then picked him up and brought him over to the ticket counter.

"One resident ticket, please." I handed my license to the woman inside the ticket booth. Even though residents of Wisteria Falls got into the botanical gardens for free, we still needed a ticket.

As she keyed in my information, I noticed a small sign about the missing cow taped in the bottom corner of the glass window separating us. Along with its picture and the warning to not approach the cow on one's own was the number of where to call if he was spotted. I'd been all too familiar with that phone number lately. The Wisteria Falls Police Department.

After another moment, the printer spit out one ticket, and the woman at the counter slid it toward me. She looked familiar, but I couldn't put my finger on why. Although Wisteria Falls was a small town, I didn't know everyone by name but knew that they were from town if recognizable.

"You getting any sightings out here?" I asked, nodding to the sign.

"Only one or two, and one was from a three-year-old little girl who kept saying *cow* and pointing to the woods. They were from out of town and didn't know about him, but they reported it at the desk just in case. I don't think they had believed their daughter. Probably thought it was a moose. They were wicked surprised when I confirmed she was right and said I'd call for a patrol to go up there. It turned up nothing, though. Would be nice to find him before it gets cold."

"I'll keep my eyes peeled."

"And so will I," Trubbs said.

Remembering my conversation with him at the car, I leaned forward, a Cheshire cat grin on my face. "My cat wanted me to ask you if the leash law also applied to him."

"I did no such thing," Trubbs retorted with a loud meow.

The woman did a double take at the cat in my arms. "Well now, that's a question I've never gotten before." She thought a moment. "I take it he's well trained."

"Like you wouldn't believe." I scratched at the side of his neck. "He listens to commands really well, and sometimes he even gives me his own."

She chuckled. "Got a talker, hmm? I have one that does that too. Always lets me know when it's dinnertime. Breakfast too. Best alarm clock I've ever had, though he's been messed up all summer with my youngest son home from college. Tries to get a second breakfast since my son is up earlier than I am." She shook her head slowly, one side of her lips turned up in a smile. "But he should probably stay on a leash for the sake of the birds just in case."

Trubbs harrumphed, the noise coming out almost like a sneeze.

The woman gazed fondly at him, then squinted her eyes and studied him. "Wasn't he the cat at Gio's funeral?"

"He was actually."

"Oh, he was just so darling sitting there like that in his cute little bow tie. Both my boys thought so."

"That settles it. I'm gonna have to get more," Trubbs quipped. I needed a good-paying job if he was going to insist on being so stylish.

But now I could place the woman. "You're Adam's mom, aren't you?"

"I am."

"It took me until you mentioned the funeral to figure out

where I knew you from. Obviously, I've seen you around town, but we've never really been introduced. How's your other son's arm?"

"Thankfully he doesn't need surgery for it, but he'll be going back to school with the cast still on." She raised her eyes to the ceiling. "Boys."

Trubbs squirmed in my arms. "Would you mind putting me down now?"

"Oh, I should let you two go," Adam's mom said with a dismissive wave. "If he's anything like my cat, he doesn't like being restrained for long. Go on now and enjoy."

"Thank you. It was good to see you again, this time under better circumstances."

She nodded. "You as well."

We turned away from the window and headed up the long path toward the top of the gardens and the wisteria falls. Because I'd been here recently, I already had photos from the shorter path of the various scenic spots.

A third of the way up the hill and a few dozen photos later, Trubbs pranced at my side, occasionally stopping to smell the flowers.

"Hang on, Trubbs," I said as he approached a pink flower. "Let me see if you can get close to those." The last thing I wanted to do was to have him smell something he shouldn't. I pulled up a flower ID app I'd downloaded to help me at Mrs. Roland's shop and prepared to snap a photo of the pretty plant.

"This one's fine," he replied calmly. "I remember seeing these out on the tables at the cat café. You know they wouldn't let anyone bring in anything that wasn't good for us."

"You know flowers too?" That made me feel better, but I still wanted to check it just in case. I took a quick picture of a nearby flower while he wasn't looking. "Maybe I should start bringing you to the florist to help me."

"I don't know their names. Just how they look."

"Gotcha. Well, it's not like I have an actual job there anyway. That all depends on if Mrs. Roland decides to hire me."

His tail twitched as he shoved his face into the flower. A zinnia, so safe for him. "I wouldn't be able to go to work with you, though. Some things would definitely be dangerous for me there."

It's a good thing I'd only been joking because he had a point. Things like lilies, common in so many arrangements, were deadly to cats. Mrs. Roland had warned me multiple times about it during my first day there and again before I headed home. I'd gone so far as to put the clothes I'd worn that day in a bag, separate from the rest of the things in my hamper, to keep Trubbs safe. With how much he liked to lie in my dirty clothes, I wasn't taking any chances.

I let the leash out as far as it would go and locked it before lifting my camera to my face. As Trubbs investigated the flowers, I took several photos of him. Flat on the ground, the slack leash barely showed in the photos, and his harness popped against his fur.

Trubbs wandered away from the zinnias a moment later to follow a butterfly fluttering along the path. With a quick click of a button, the slack on his leash retracted as he pursued the winged beauty.

I continued snapping away with my camera. My followers were going to love these.

When the butterfly stopped on a different flower, Trubbs got down low.

"Trubbs, leave it. I don't know what those flowers are."

He didn't listen and crouched even closer to the ground, his ears pulling back and his bum wiggling.

I hastily grabbed my cell to pull up the phone app to identify the flower but wasn't fast enough. The butterfly lifted back into the air, and Trubbs launched himself, only to trigger the leash's auto-lock that worked much like a seatbelt.

"Hey, I would have had that." He looked over his shoulder and glared at me.

"Sorry. Feature of the leash. I wasn't expecting it either. But I bet the butterfly is happy to be free to continue on its fluttery way." To appease him, I added, "You absolutely would have had it."

He harrumphed once more, flicking his tail at me as he started back up the path.

It was a beautiful day. Midweek and not crowded. Perfect for Trubbs's first outing. Only a handful of other visitors passed us going up or down. Most paused at least briefly, and Trubbs, people pleaser and attention lover that he was, happily rubbed against their legs and let them pet him for as long as they liked. Some then followed me on social media to stay connected to my purrfect traveling companion.

Three quarters of the way to the top, I could tell Trubbs was getting tired. We pulled off to the side of the path and onto a bench set up at a scenic overlook. The spot had gorgeous views of the wisteria spilling into the lake below. I grabbed my good camera and took several pictures while Trubbs soaked in the sun on the warm bench, then I switched to my cell to take a selfie. The wisteria made for a beautiful background. Once he felt up to it, I'd ask Trubbs if he'd take one with me. If not, my followers would have to be satisfied with a cat basking in the warm sunlight.

"Only thing that would make this better is a snack," Trubbs purred with a stretch.

"I can help with that." I dug into my backpack to find the treats I'd packed. "Here." I set two treats in front of him, then went back into my bag for a bottle of water and a bowl. Setting the bowl down where the treats had been, I then cracked open the water and poured some for him.

As I sipped at what remained in the bottle, Trubbs lapped at the drink but kept turning away and making the cutest strange face with each lick.

"What's wrong?" I asked, trying to hide the amusement from my voice.

"It's too bright." He tapped at the dish.

Now I felt bad for almost laughing. "I'm so sorry." I moved his water to a shadier portion of the bench. I'd have to look into getting a travel bowl and not his spare metal dish that we usually used at home.

"You should have said you didn't like it there as soon as you realized." Not for the first time, I appreciated how lucky I was that he could talk. How much longer would it have taken me to realize what his problem was? "Try again. It's in the shade now."

He'd lowered his head about halfway to the dish when he shot up straight and stood against the back of the bench.

"What's going on?"

"Sh . . . Don't you hear that?" He stared out into the woodsy area beyond the flower field.

"Nope." I gazed out in that direction but saw nothing either.

His ears twitched. "There it is again."

I'd have to take his word for it. Cats heard and saw better than humans. But that didn't stop me from looking into the woods as he jumped off the bench and crossed the path to get a closer look. He stood up on his hind legs, the leash going taut as he pulled at it.

"Trubbs, how about we start walking again? We're almost to the top."

"Hang on. There it is!"

"What?"

"The cow!"

Before I could process what he was doing, Trubbs scooted back across the path and under the bench, pulling the leash tight in front of him.

And then he was off, darting away from me toward the woods.

Chapter Thirty-Three

I stood holding Trubbs's slack leash attached to a now empty harness. I didn't know whether to be annoyed or impressed by how quickly he got it off.

"Trubbs!" I called after him as he bounded into the woods.

Pausing only long enough to dump the water bowl and take it with me before weaving my way through the various flowers and shrubs, I followed Trubbs as best as I could. The sign had said not to chase the cow if it were spotted, but it said nothing about chasing after your cat after he saw said cow.

Of course, between my cautiousness about not trampling the plants and Trubbs's several seconds' head start, I could no longer see my cat and instead was following him in what I hoped was the right direction based on the sound of him rustling through the flora.

But all too soon, I couldn't hear him either.

"Trubbs?"

Nothing.

Then maybe something. A stick snapped in the distance,

and I turned toward it and walked further into the woods. I continued to follow every larger noise I heard. Probably not the smartest decision in hindsight.

After several minutes, I could no longer see the flower-filled gardens through the trees when I turned around.

I should have stayed put. That's what they said to do when lost.

But was I lost?

Okay, yes, I was.

I didn't know if I was even within the boundaries of the botanical gardens anymore.

And as much as I liked to travel, I had no innate sense of north and south or east and west either. I was going to need a compass if I went on any real hikes with Trubbs. If I let him come anywhere with me after this.

"Trubbs? Trouble!"

Now I couldn't hear anything but the birds in the trees above me.

I turned around, hoping that if this way lacked noise, going in the opposite direction would have me finding my cat or the cow or both.

Instead, a few more minutes found me literally stumbling onto a narrow path after tripping on an unseen branch. I was glad I hadn't fallen on my face. No doubt it would have left a mark. That would have been hard to explain to Jay, though he'd probably find much of this amusing as long as I wasn't trespassing on someone else's property right now. Breaking the law would probably complicate my dating a cop. Hopefully he didn't mind my cat violating the leash law.

I turned left on the path, and within a minute, not only had I stepped in what I believed to be a cow pie (gross!), but I'd stumbled—this time not literally—onto something much bigger.

But I still didn't know where I was, and Trubbs was nowhere in sight. I pulled out my phone and hoped Jay would be awake by now as I pressed the call button.

After two rings, Jay picked up. "Mer?" He still sounded a little tired, but if he'd answered, I hadn't woken him. "Was about to hop in the shower, what's up?"

The words rushed out of me. "I was walking my cat, and he got loose, and I think I found where the cow's been, and I may have just figured out Gio's murder. But now I don't see my cat or the cow, and I've stepped in poo, and I don't know where I am."

"Whoa, whoa, whoa. Slow down." Jay was now wide awake from the sounds of it.

I took a deep breath. "I'm in trouble. I'm lost and I need your help."

"Tell me where I should look for you. I'll call Owens, and did you say the cow? The missing cow?"

"Uh-huh. Near the botanical gardens. Three quarters of the way up the long side. Woods behind the bench." That was the best I could do.

"Okay. I'll call the station and get them there with the trailer too. It won't take me long. Stay where you are. I'm coming."

CHAPTER THIRTY-FOUR

Stay where I was. Not a problem. I wasn't moving from this spot. For one, I didn't want to get lost any more than I was. And two, I wasn't sure if I'd be able to find this spot if I walked away from it again.

A million things raced through my mind as I surveyed the scene in front of me. Plastic littered the area, but not just any plastic. The clear cellophane wrapping that would surround a bouquet. Nearest to my foot was a fragment of plastic that still had the sticker from Mrs. Roland's shop on it that featured her logo.

It wasn't the only logo sticker I could see. Fragments of others still attached to cellophane poked out from the leaves. The area was well-trampled with cow pies scattered through-out, but it also looked like someone had tried to turn the leaves over to hide the bouquets.

I could think of only one person who would do this. One person who had bouquets to hide.

Floyd.

This whole time, he'd been taking the bouquets from Mrs.

Roland's shop, the ones Gio had bought and paid for, and burying them in the woods. No wonder the cow was hanging out here. He had an ample supply of food from the botanical gardens and got a treat every week in the form of the bouquets that were supposed to go to Naomi. Was this why Trubbs had said that Floyd's shoes smelled funny? Had he stepped in a cow pie up here like I had? He must have been coming here each week to hide the bouquets, so it was certainly possible.

No offense to the cow, but what a waste of beautiful flowers. Floyd could have given them to the hospital or nursing home instead. At least there, they would have provided someone with some cheering up.

Mrs. Roland would not be happy about this, but at least she'd no longer have a murderer working for her.

And Floyd probably called for the pizza he picked up for him and Naomi after leaving the flowers here, then would arrive back home with it still steaming hot. Given the route I knew he had to take to get from here to there, the timing worked out.

A lot of things did. I just hoped Jay would see it this time. There was a hole in his alibi somewhere. There had to be.

"Meredith!!" Jay called. His voice was distant, but not so far away either.

I pivoted toward the noise and raised my hands, swinging them wildly overhead. "Jay! I'm over here!"

He only needed to yell one more time before I spotted him running toward me in regular street clothes and not his uniform.

"Meredith!" Trubbs bounded past Jay. "I lost the cow, and then you weren't at the bench when I went back."

He reached me with Jay still out of earshot as he wound

his way through the trees as quickly as the underbrush would let him.

I stooped to pick him up. "You really think I'd just sit and wait for you? The cow could have trampled you!"

"It would do no such thing. He's scared."

"They charge when scared."

"He ran the other way," Trubbs replied with a flick of his tail, then considered this another moment as he crawled into my arms. "Besides, I can climb trees, remember? He'd never get to me up there. Not here."

I hugged him. "Well, please don't go giving him another opportunity."

"He's not sure if he'll stick around."

"I thought you said you lost him."

"Yeah, he ran away when I said people were looking for him."

Jay was now about fifteen feet away.

"Watch out for the cow pies!" I called out.

He slowed his pace, but only a little as he scanned the ground before placing each foot. "Trubbs was standing on the path right at the spot where you said he'd gotten loose. Gave us a solid spot to start looking for you." He finally reached me and pulled me in for a hug. "How are you doing?"

"I'm okay. Better now that you both found me."

Trubbs squirmed between us. "Okay, that's enough hugging."

Jay stepped back with a crooked grin and rubbed the back of his neck. "Sorry for squishing you there, Trouble."

"He's polite, I'll give him that," Trubbs said as he pulled himself up and onto my shoulder, then used the small backpack I was wearing as a seat.

It was then I realized Jay was alone, not that I minded. (Preferred it, actually.) "Where's Owens?"

"Standing by the bench and running point with the guys and the cow trailer. Should probably call him." He pulled out his cell and, within seconds, was talking to Owens. I doubted it had rung more than once on Owens's end, if at all. "Yeah, I found her . . . No there's no sign of the cow, but he's been here . . . Dunno yet. Was gonna wait to have her fill me in when you get here . . . About fifty yards or so straight in, then northeast about another twenty, but you'll see us."

I was less than a football field away from the path? Ugh, how embarrassing.

Jay clicked off the call. "He'll be here in a minute."

I couldn't wait until Owens got here to fill in Jay. "Floyd did it. I'm sure of it."

"He has an alibi."

"Is it a good one? Airtight? Witnesses?"

"Naomi, for one."

I didn't want to think that she'd lie for him. Not with knowing what I did. But it was a possibility. "You know that's not the greatest. They're together."

He made a face. "Timestamps on the highway. Hotel check-in time."

"People speed. How much time do you think it took to kill Gio?" I held up my hand. "Don't answer that."

By this time Owens—also not in uniform—was within eye sight. He let out a loud *ugh*.

Oops. "Watch out for the cow pies," I belatedly warned him. I returned my attention to Jay. "Did you ask anyone in town if they saw him leave in the van?"

"He said he didn't see anyone."

My eyes widened. "That's not what he told me."

Owens crossed his arms as he came to a stop beside Jay. "What did he tell you?"

"He mentioned seeing the regular morning joggers, dog

walkers, and even a guy with a . . . skateboard." I tried to shake the thought away, but it refused to budge. Yet I was missing something.

"Looks like we'll be calling him back in." He gestured to the trampled area behind me. "How does this tie in?"

I toed the label near my foot. "Notice something familiar, Jay?"

"This is from my mom's shop."

"And there's more where this came from." I pointed and explained about how Gio had been sending flowers to Naomi since their divorce but that she hadn't gotten them since she and Floyd got together. "My guess is he's been dumping them here. Who would notice if random flower petals blew in from the woods?"

Owens humphed. "Not very smart to leave it in the plastic. Guess we could pick him up on illegal dumping and follow through on the murder charges after that with more evidence. Too bad we couldn't pull any prints from the scene."

"Gio was a stickler about cleanliness," I said, knowing all too well how much so. "You'd think the stainless in there was fingerprint resistant, but it wasn't."

"Probably all the flour," Owens stated dismissively.

I shook my head. "Flour's great for leaving fingerprints. Sticks and gets all over the place. The killer had to have been wearing gloves." A weight settled in my stomach. That was it. "I don't think it was Floyd."

Owens furrowed his brows. "But you just said—"

"I know what I said. I was wrong. But I do know who it is."

"Are you seriously going to let a citizen dictate our investigation, Roland?" Owens turned, but I still caught his eye roll. "Come on, let's go get Mr. Bailey for dumping and lean on him about the murder. Always thought he had a strong motive."

"And he did. He didn't like that Gio continued to give Naomi flowers even after she started going out with him. That's why he started dumping them. He wasn't happy to find out Gio had prepaid and Naomi would still be getting flowers for several more months either. But Floyd didn't do it. He saw who did, though."

Owens humphed again.

Jay eyed his partner. "We should hear her out, Owens. Go ahead, Mer."

"The guy on the skateboard did it."

Owens raised his eyebrow and drew his lips into a tight line. "He could be anyone."

"But the skatepark is in the opposite direction of the bakery, so if I'm right about who Floyd saw, then this skate-boarder was not where he should have been had he been going to the skatepark from home like he said he was. And he also wasn't wearing his skateboarding gloves a short time later, which could have prevented him from breaking his wrist that morning when he fell off his skateboard."

Jay's eyes grew wide. "If he even fell off the skateboard."

"You're getting it now, aren't you?" He nodded. "And he would have locked the bakery door too. I thought it was Floyd because he's not from here and still locks your mom's van at night, but Ryan's been away at college. I always locked my door there. Took me a while to get back into the small-town mindset of not needing to."

"They have a cat too," Trubbs reminded me with a head butt to the top of my head.

Not having forgotten, I reached up and scratched his side. That was going to be my next point. "And they have a cat who has been getting up early with him."

"How do you know that last part?" Owens asked, sounding slightly less skeptical.

"His mom just told me. She's the one selling the tickets here right now. I'd be willing to bet it matches the fur you found."

Jay held up his hand. "We already know it does from when we looked into his brother."

Owens turned to Jay. "Way to go telling her more facts about the case."

"You mentioned the lack of fingerprints." Jay shrugged. "If she helps solve this case, I don't care what she knows. She gave us enough to bring him in for questions."

"Wait, it's Wednesday."

Owens raised an eyebrow. "What of it?"

Understandably he didn't know, being new to town, but Jay figured it out immediately. "Trash day for half the town." He pulled out his phone, then his fingers flew over the screen as he typed.

"From Main Street through to the skatepark. Wanna make a bet one of the town barrels has a pair of flour-covered skateboarding gloves in it?"

"Owens, get someone to come process this scene. Then we can grab our suspects." Someone on the other end of the call must have picked up. "It's Roland. I need the contents from all the barrels between Flour Power and the skatepark bagged for evidence . . . Yeah, not anymore. If the truck's already picked some up, we'll need the truck's contents too."

Once he was done doing what Jay had told him, Owens looked at the sky, slowly shaking his head. "I can't believe my day off was canceled because of a cat and a cow."

"And possibly solving a murder. Can't forget that," I reminded him.

"Hey, at least you didn't have plans," Jay added, slipping

his phone back into his pocket. He reached for my hand. "Dennis is handling the trash collection, but we're probably stuck sorting through it. I'm sorry I'm going to have to call off our date this evening. No way will I finish with all of this before then."

Owens groaned as I squeezed Jay's hand. "That's okay. Another time."

"We can figure that out once you come in."

"Once I come in?" I repeated.

"Yeah. We're gonna need your official statement on all of this."

"Got it. Maybe I could bring you lunch?"

Jay smiled. "I'd like that."

Owens humphed once more. Seemed to be his go-to.

"I'll get you lunch too, Officer Owens. My thanks for solving Gio's murder."

For the first time since meeting him, he cracked a smile. "All right. Well, I'll stay at the scene until someone gets up here." He turned to Jay. "You go walk Miss Duffy and her cat back to her car. That can be your date. But make it quick."

Jay didn't need to be told twice. He dropped my hand, allowing him to come up to my side, his arm extended for me to wrap mine through.

"You going to be good up there, Trubbs?" I peered up at the cat still using my backpack as a seat.

He stretched out, sliding his front paws forward and down until he was draped over my shoulder. "Should be good now."

With that, the three of us made our way out of the woods, leaving Owens to photograph the scene from where he stood while he waited for backup.

"Think Owens is questioning his move to Wisteria Falls after all of this?" I asked when we reached the path a few minutes later.

Jay laughed as we turned up the hill. "Nah. He's thrilled that one of his first cases is a murder. Told him not to get used to it."

"Yeah, let's hope not. You know you took us the long way, right?"

"Sure do," he said, his mouth curling into a grin. "Owens doesn't know that, though."

I lay my head against Jay's upper arm, almost reaching his shoulder.

Trubbs dug his grip into me, "Whoa, whoa, whoa."

I quickly lifted my head so he could regain his balance. I did not want him to fall off me again. Not with those sharp claws.

When we reached the topmost overlook, Jay pulled away from me. "Hand me your phone."

No questions asked, I did as he requested.

"Let me take a picture of you and Trouble."

"I like him," Trubbs said as I picked out a place to stand.

"So do I." And it was true, making me more bummed out about our date being postponed than I had been already. But postponed wasn't the same thing as canceled, and we had right now. Besides, the delay was hopefully happening for the best reason. Capturing Gio's killer.

"Okay, now smile, you two," Jay said as he held up my phone. Trubbs bumped his head against the side of my face. "Whoops, took a selfie. Let's try that again."

The second time, he was successful. He handed me my phone as I reached him. I immediately looked in my gallery to find the accidental shot. Teasingly, I said, "I might have to make this my contact photo for you."

He groaned, despite my obvious jest. It wasn't a great photo. Not centered, his chin and right ear cut off, his face serious. Very unlike the Jay I knew.

"Nah, I have a better idea." I pulled him to where I'd been standing with Trubbs and held the phone out in front of us in selfie mode. As I was about to press the button to capture the photo, I turned quickly and kissed Jay on the cheek.

He placed his hand in that spot as I pulled away, eager to look at the picture and a little embarrassed at having been so bold. But looking at the photo of the two of us—well, three if you counted Trubbs and his photobomb—I was glad I'd made the move. Jay's eyes were wide but twinkling, and his grin was one of absolute contentment.

"This one is going to be your contact photo," I said as he came up behind me.

"Now that one I like." He took my hand in his, and we walked back down from the falls on the short side. When we reached my car, he tried to apologize once more about having to push our date back.

"I don't know what you're talking about," I replied. "This seemed like a pretty good first date to me. How many other girls get to say they helped solve a murder?"

Jay kissed the top of my head. "Oof, just set a pretty high bar with that, didn't we? I hope I'll be able to top it next time."

"You will. Now go get Gio's killer."

CHAPTER THIRTY-FIVE

I'd stayed up later than I had in a long time, hoping I'd get a call from Jay, that he'd tell me I'd been right about who killed Gio and that they'd gotten a full confession from him.

No such call came.

While I waited, I worked on my blog, choosing to write a post on the trip to the Wisteria Falls Botanical Gardens with Trubbs rather than one of the other places I still had in my backlog. I'd get to those eventually, but the trip with Trubbs allowed me to try out my new type of content for the first time—traveling with my purrfect travel companion. After all, it was what my influx of followers was here for.

My following had continued to climb since the rebranding, and my comments and inbox were flooded by other travelers and adventurers who took their pets on the road with them. Some lived in RVs, others hiked in the wilderness, and even more had only done one big trip or move with their pet, but all of them wished me well in this endeavor.

I loved this community already.

And let's face it, working on this specific blog post gave

me an extra reason to look at the picture of Jay and me again. I had it bad. Funny how quickly and easily one could go all in from not realizing those feelings even existed.

"Are you coming to bed yet?" Trubbs asked about two hours after I'd usually be in my room asleep. "I've been keeping your pillow warm."

"Yeah. Just want to finish going through the last of these comments." And give Jay (or even Owens at this rate) a chance to call with an update.

But once I was done with deleting spam and responding to genuine messages without hearing from anyone, I followed Trubbs to bed.

I awoke in the morning to Trubbs tapping my nose. "Your phone keeps lighting up, and I don't know what to do."

"What do you mean?" I reached over for the phone on my nightstand. It wasn't there. "Where's my phone?"

He backed up a few steps as I pulled myself up to a sitting position. "On the floor. I *may* have knocked it down this morning while trying to turn off your alarm."

I rubbed my eyes. "You turned off my alarm?" What time was it?

Trubbs flicked his tail. "You were up late and needed your sleep. It wasn't like you were going anywhere until lunchtime."

"Didn't you need breakfast?" He looked away. "Trubbs, did you have breakfast?"

"I took care of it." I didn't know if I wanted to know what that meant. "But now your phone is lighting up."

"Must be a phone call." Wait. I lunged over the side of my bed to retrieve my phone, practically falling out of bed as I did. It was lighting up again as I struggled to right myself among my now tangled sheets. "Hello?"

Mrs. Roland's frantic tone greeted me. "Oh, Meredith. I'm so glad you finally picked up. Is everything okay?"

"Yeah, everything's fine—"

"Thank heavens. Jay didn't come home last night, and then when I called him, he's at work and can't talk. Then Floyd didn't come in today with no explanation, and I can't reach him or Naomi, so it's been quite the morning. I'm really in a bind and was hoping you could come help me today, but if something happened with your date last night and it's too weird . . ."

"There was no date, actually. Work stuff. So sure." I extricated myself from my mess of sheets and set my feet on the ground. "Give me a chance to get ready and I'll come in, but I'm going to need a long lunch break if that's okay. I told Jay I'd bring him something since we had to reschedule."

Much more relieved, she said, "I will take whatever time you can give me. I'll see you when you get here." With that, she hung up the phone, leaving me to get ready for work and prep lunch as best I could before needing to go.

I'd been aware of every second of the morning's passing as I worked with Mrs. Roland, doing my best to not spill what I knew about everything going on. About why Jay had gone to work on his day off, why Floyd hadn't come in, and why he and Naomi weren't answering their phones. I could only imagine what Naomi knew and how she was feeling about it.

But finally it was lunchtime. Before I left to help Mrs. Roland, I'd raided my parents' chest freezer in the basement for Mom's meatballs and put them in the slow cooker with a quickly thrown together homemade sauce. On the way home to grab the food, I'd stopped at the grocery store for some fresh bread. It pained me to go there—not because it was bad, but because it wasn't Flour Power—but I had no other option, especially not with the limited time I had.

I sliced open the rolls, loaded up the meatballs and sauce, then topped them with provolone cheese. For a finishing touch, I sprinkled on some of my own garlic bread seasoning on top of it all and set the grinders to broil until the cheese was nice and melted. The garlic was probably going a bit overboard considering where they worked and how many people they talked to, but oh well. It was too late.

Trubbs was waiting for me when I got outside with lunch.

"I wanted to wish you good luck today. I hope everything is settled now."

He'd been staying clear of me since I'd discovered what he'd meant by his having taken care of breakfast. Dry kibble everywhere. How he got into the cupboard this time, I didn't know, but there was a mess of kitty crunchies scattered across my floor this morning, the bag on its side still half in the cupboard.

"Thanks, Trubbs. Lunch is waiting in there for you."

"I'm good. Thank you." He shook his head, almost as if fighting off a sneeze. "The smell you cooked up is not my favorite. And I think I ate too much this morning."

I'd have to remember that he wasn't a fan of garlic. "And knowing that, I don't want to know how much was originally on my floor. Which is now clean, by the way. All evidence of this morning's breakfast heist has been taken care of."

"You cleaned it up?" If cats dropped their mouths in shock, I believed he would have right then.

"I couldn't let it stay all over my floor."

"I was going to eat that!"

"How was I supposed to know? You left in a hurry this morning."

"You've seen me do it." He dropped his head.

"Your days of having to eat food directly off the floor are gone, Trubbs. I hope you know that."

He walked up to me and wound himself between my feet. "I still would have eaten it."

"I know." Careful not to drop the sandwiches, I squatted to pet my unique feline friend. "The windows are open, so hopefully the smell will clear out for you soon."

"Thanks." He spun around and trotted off into the neighbor's yard . . . with my nosy neighbor, Dolores, standing in it staring at me.

I waved.

She eyed me skeptically. "He's a chatty one. Almost like he was having a real conversation with you."

"Maybe he is in his own way." I shrugged. "He likes it when I talk to him. Have a good day!"

No doubt my mother would hear about this, but she knew all about Trubbs's talkative habits. Well, except for the fact he could actually talk.

I couldn't worry about that now, though. I had lunch to deliver and, hopefully, good news to receive.

Chapter Thirty-Six

As soon as Dennis saw me enter the station, he whisked me away past the waiting reporters, including my best friend. Although I quickly waved at her, I was grateful it looked like I was only there to deliver lunch, not to give a statement as well. She'd find out soon enough. Either Jay would slip or I'd spill. Even so, she eyed the bag of sandwiches and raised and lowered her eyebrows several times before I was ushered out of view.

"Busy today," I commented.

Dennis snorted jovially. "I have it under good authority that you're a big reason why."

"Me? Never. No, I'm just here to deliver lunch."

He led me to an office. "The other rooms we'd take you to are full, so sit tight and someone will be in to take your statement."

Nodding, I hadn't missed that he didn't say Jay or Owens. Though, they were probably still busy with all of this. If Jay hadn't been able to talk to his mom earlier, then they had to be. He always made time for her.

Fifteen minutes later, Tony appeared. His gaze homed in on the takeout containers. "You bring me any?"

I shook my head. "Sorry. Should have thought of that." I'd have to remember him and Dennis next time. If there was a next time. I hoped there would be a next time. Just not one that also saw me having to give a statement.

He cracked a smile. "I'm just jokin'. If you go giving us all lunch, what are we gonna tease Jay about?"

"I brought some for Owens too."

His brows furrowed momentarily. "Well, that's nice of you. After their night, I'm sure they're looking forward to it. That and a nap."

"Will they be much longer?"

"Not sure." He sat in the seat across from me. "I'm here to take your statement."

Tony got set up, then I recounted everything that had happened yesterday regarding my finding the dumping site. Unable to say that Trubbs had seen the cow, I played off my discovery of the cow's presence as happenstance to Trubbs running off and suggested that maybe he'd gone after the steer. Once he was done and the recorder turned off, I realized none of the questions had been related to the murder. As I went to ask him why, he set up a second recorder. The questions were fewer and pertained to my conversation with Ryan, Adam, and their mom at the funeral home, and my conversation with Floyd the night he got back from the flower show when he'd said he'd seen someone on a skateboard.

"Most of everything is all hearsay from you," Tony admitted after he turned off the recorder. "But it's good corroboration for what else we've got."

"So you got him? Ryan confessed?"

"Why don't I show you?" He opened the desk drawer, then after a moment of shuffling papers, he pulled out a remote and pressed a button. The television mounted in the upper corner of the room flared to life. Tony pressed another button, and the screen flickered to the local news where the anchors were sitting at the desk in front of a screen displaying *Breaking News* across it in big red letters. They cut to Rita standing outside the station.

"I'm here in Wisteria Falls where a press conference in the next few minutes is expected to reveal that there's been a major break in the murder of local business owner and baker Giovanni Pinelli, the first murder in the town in over two decades."

"She's great at what she does, isn't she?" Tony said about Rita, his tone full of admiration, when it went to commercial.

"Made for TV." Growing up, I'd always thought it would be more sitcom or TV drama, but joining the high school newspaper and then taking an elective in college sent her down the broadcasting path.

"Well, I have to go deliver these." He held up the recorders. "They should be in as soon as the conference is over."

"Thanks, Tony. Good to see ya again."

He ducked out of the room, leaving me to watch the press conference alone. As often as I saw Rita on TV, this was one of the few times I'd ever seen Jay on the small screen. The last time was probably in high school on a football game highlights reel. Seeing him like this? Shining in the moment as he announced the suspect in Gio's murder had confessed? He'd never looked so good. The uniform helped too, of course.

I learned several things while watching the press conference. Ryan hadn't planned on killing Gio that day, but he had gone to the bakery to talk to him. He was there to pick up his brother's check. Adam had thought it would be best if he didn't go get it. Turned out Gio had mailed it like Adam told me at the funeral home. It got to his house later that day. Gio saying he mailed it should have been the end, but instead, the exchange got heated. Somehow, they'd already knocked over the flour, so when Ryan pushed Gio, Gio slipped and ultimately met his demise. In a panic, Ryan had tried to cover his tracks, spreading even more flour on the counter and floor but leaving a partial footprint in his wake. The strange mark in the flour had been from padding on his skateboarding gloves, which he disposed of on his way to the skatepark and had been recovered by Jay and Owens. His accident at the skatepark was an attempt to create his alibi that had gone too far. Breaking his board and calling his brother had been the plan, not breaking his arm.

Whether Adam knew what happened before today's news conference or if he had been helping to cover for his brother, I wasn't certain. No doubt that would be revealed eventually. Either way, I couldn't imagine being in his shoes.

About a half hour after the press conference ended, Jay and Owens strolled into the office. Owens seemed pleased, but Jay's face only brightened when he saw me.

I stood and approached him, my arms wide. "You looked very handsome up there."

He walked into my waiting hug. "Saw that, huh?"

"Mm-hmm. Thank you for catching Gio's killer. I'm glad, but it's bittersweet."

"I understand. We feel the same way. Most of us here on the force were still kids the last time one happened. It brought a lot of excitement to the station, but, wow, Gio." He gave me another squeeze before stepping back and holding me out at arm's length. "You, however, broke this case wide open."

"I did?"

Owens cleared his throat. "Yeah. We never would have

known to look at Ryan Chambers had it not been for you revealing what Mr. Bailey told you about seeing the suspect on his skateboard that morning."

"But I wouldn't have said anything had I not been so incorrectly sure that Floyd had been the one to kill Gio." Thank goodness for that cow leading me to the flowers. And for Trubbs spotting the cow in the first place. "It was a group effort. Thank you for solving the murder too, Officer Owens."

He cracked a smile. "Please, call me Patrick."

I nodded, glad I'd finally made headway with Jay's partner who had once considered me a suspect. "Can't guarantee that it's all that hot anymore, but I brought lunch." I pointed to the bag of grinders on the desk.

"That's all right," Jay replied. "We've been going since you called us yesterday with barely a break. It's going to be the best lunch ever."

And in some ways, it was.

CHAPTER THIRTY-SEVEN

A few days had passed since Ryan was charged with Gio's murder, but losing Gio and the unknown future of Flour Power would be felt for some time to come. Last I'd heard, his family hadn't gone over his will yet. If he even had one. I hoped, for the town's sake, that the bakery wouldn't be empty for long.

Things were settling down throughout Wisteria Falls. The reporters—all but Rita, who lived here—had gone home. The biggest news in town was once again the missing cow. Several patrols had gone up there since Trubbs had spotted him, but he was still evading capture. There had been more signs of him hanging around the botanical gardens, however, and to be better prepared, the trailer that would eventually transport him to a sanctuary sat waiting for him in the parking lot. Trubbs seemed concerned about him, and I promised him we'd go back to the gardens to try to find him. Together. No running off without me nonsense.

As for me? I had a job. Sort of.

"Have a good day, Trubbs," I called after my cat as he

sauntered away from the front door of the florist. He'd taken to walking me to work in the morning before going off and doing whatever it was he did during the day.

The bell above the door chimed as I pushed it open, announcing my arrival. "Good morning, Meredith."

"Morning, Mrs. Roland. What do we have today?"

"Oh, the usual, but I'll need you to drop off flowers to Naomi on your way home tonight if you don't mind. I trust that *you'll* get them there."

"Of course."

Mrs. Roland had not been happy to find out that Floyd had been trashing the bouquets they'd been making for Naomi each week.

For his illegal dumping at the botanical gardens, Floyd had entered a plea deal and been sentenced to community service throughout the town. He took it without complaint. It probably helped his case that it was his eyewitness testimony that put Ryan at the scene of Gio's murder. Not that the general public knew that. Yet. Word would no doubt spread throughout town sooner or later.

Floyd hadn't quite lost his job—despite what happened, Mrs. Roland liked him too much to fire him and knew it wouldn't happen again—but there were stipulations to his coming back that he still had to meet. Finishing his community service was one of them. At two hundred hours, it was going to take him at least five weeks to complete it. So I was employed until then if not longer, filling in at the flower shop.

There was no telling how long the other part would take. Naomi's forgiveness. She'd kicked him out after learning what he'd done, and he'd been back with his parents since then. I figured I'd get a feel for how things were going when I made my delivery tonight.

After that, I was heading home for a night in with Trubbs.

And tomorrow? Well, tomorrow night was date night. Finally.

All in all, things were going well. Purrfect Travel Companion was taking off, so much so that offers of free tickets to area attractions and beyond were coming in for both me and Trubbs. Some places wanted to highlight their being pet-friendly, and others wanted to try it out and get some publicity in the process.

Perhaps it would soon be time for a vacation after all.

Meredith and Trubbs will return in *Catastrophe on a Cruise*. They better start packing.
In the meantime, continue your stay in Fiddlefern Fjord, home to Wisteria Falls, Heartwood Hollow, and more with one of Rosie's other cozy books.

What's Next?

Looking for a new mystery featuring several cats and kittens who have a lot to say? *Foster Familiar,* Book 1 of the Feline Familiar Cat Cafe series has got you covered... in cat hair!

Curious about Joanie, that baker in Heartwood Hollow? She's a matchmaking baker living in a town that's full of secrets. Start to uncover them in *Cookies and Curses*, Book 1 of the Mixing Up Magic series.

Foster Familiar and Cookies and Curses are both available now.